The Case of Mr. Porter and His Mouse

A Dana Sorensen Novel

Amanda Loveless

Enid, Oklahoma

ISBN: 978-0-9904470-1-6

for my parents

Table of Contents

hit you on the ass on your way out. Otherwise, take the damn file and get out of my office.'

Floretta sailed toward the door, not bothering to wait for Dana to leave first. 'Now, if you'll excuse me, staff meeting is about to start, and as much as I would like to skip it, it's the only chance I get to count bodies and make sure you people can still fog a mirror.' She turned on her heel just as she reached the door. 'By the way, how *did* it go at the school this morning?'

Dana shrugged and hauled herself to her feet. 'Well, that depends on how strong an argument you can make that a particular text messaging server is used in interstate communications.'

Floretta closed her eyes. 'So help me, Dana Sorensen, if you have violated the Computer Fraud and Abuse Act *again*, I will—'

'Relax. It's fine. I had permission. Sort of.' She scooped up the file on Floretta's desk and shoved it into her bag. 'It's not like it was a real attack. And, anyway, it's not my fault people leave their passwords in predictable places.'

'Just promise me you'll behave while you're at GES. I meant what I said. If you're serious about that promotion, you better play nice.'

Dana brushed past Floretta. 'If I decide to take this assignment, Floretta, my behavior will be the least of your worries.'

An hour later, Dana peeled off her jacket and flung herself into a booth at Marisol's, her favorite Mexican restaurant in OKC. It was the kind of place where customers seated themselves and pop was served in the can with a glass of ice but nobody cared because the tortillas were fresh, the food was mostly authentic, and the beer was cold. Colorful papel picado banners fluttered above the bent heads of hungry patrons, fat beads of sweat rolled down the sides of iced beverages, and forks clinked happily against plates. It was a good place to be.

There was already ice water on the table when she got there, along with a large plate of warm, salty tortilla chips piled around a bowl of Marisol's famous salsa. Mazie Reid, her oldest friend and colleague, was sprawled out in the opposite side of the booth, fanning herself with a paper menu.

'So tell me again why we had to come here in separate vehicles?' Mazie asked, reaching for the chips.

'Because,' Dana replied, 'I'm supposed to be at Grasslands Energy Solutions by two o'clock. Unless I decide to resign from my job, of course, in which case I'll just be going home.'

Mazie's mouth gaped. 'Are you serious?' she asked, searching Dana's face. 'Oh, my God, you *are* serious.' She didn't wait for Dana to respond before waving one of the regular servers over. 'Can we get two bottles of Carta Blanca? Thanks.' She turned back to Dana. 'This is crazy! What about the promotion?'

'Floretta is threatening to withhold her recommendation.' She sighed. 'I don't know. Maybe it doesn't matter. The people on the hiring committee know Floretta. They know what she's like.'

Mazie dropped her gaze but not before Dana saw the look on her face. She knew that look.

'What are you not telling me?'

Mazie gently cleared her throat. 'I didn't say anything before because I didn't want to jinx it.' She sat up straighter, as if to brace herself, and spoke fast. 'Max Chen has been campaigning pretty hard for the job. He seems to think he's got it in the bag.'

Dana swore violently. Max Chen. Arrogant, brown-nosing, two-faced, entitled, caffeine-addicted, brilliant son of a bitch. She trained him from nothing and he repaid her by stabbing her in the back. Campaigning hard for her job? She didn't doubt it. His knees must be so sore by now.

Dana looked around for the server who took their drink order. Now would be a good time for that beer to show up. She settled for a swig of water. 'And here I thought this day couldn't get any better.'

'Don't worry about Max. Would you really leave BDS?'

Dana thought about that. After fourteen years at the company, it was difficult to imagine anything else. She'd grown up in the business, watched it grow up around her. She could never be satisfied reviewing audit logs day in and day out any more than she could be satisfied living in a city apartment but something had to change. She had to change. What would she do if she didn't get the job?

'I don't know,' she said at last. 'But I'm not walking off the job today and Floretta knows it.' She wiped the cool condensation off her water glass with a paper napkin and pressed it against the back of her neck. 'I just wish I knew what Bob was up to. Flo said he specifically asked for me, if you can believe that.'

'Bob?' Mazie gave a low whistle. 'Wow. I haven't heard that

name in forever.' She snapped a tortilla chip in half and made another run at the salsa. 'To tell the truth, I still feel a little guilty about moving into his office after he left. How many years has it been now?'

Dana tossed the wet napkin on the table. Mazie was just being polite. She knew better than most just how long it had been. 'Four,' Dana reminded her. 'And if you ask me, that's not long enough.'

'So you have no idea what he wants?'

'He's asking us to cover a position until he can hire someone, or at least that's the story I got from Flo,' replied Dana, taking another swig of water. 'Why he thinks he needs me, I have no idea. I don't even know why Floretta agreed to it. It's not like he left under the best of circumstances.'

The server stopped by to drop off their beers and take their order. They went with the usual, tacos with corn tortillas and refried beans with a side of chiles en escabeche. When the server left, Mazie raised her bottle in a toast. 'To hell with all of 'em! What shall we drink to?'

'Let's go with sanity,' said Dana, clinking her bottle against Mazie's. 'Lord knows I'm going to need it.'

Mazie snorted. 'I hate to be the one to tell you this, kiddo, but I'm pretty sure that ship already sailed. Just saying.'

Bob Leroy glanced at his watch as he wheeled into the offices of the COO and President, Sam Porter. He hoped it would be a quick meeting but there was never any telling with Sam. He couldn't even guess at why he'd been summoned.

As it happened, Sam bustled out of his office just as he was about to enter. Sam was five feet tall if he was an inch and round like a pumpkin but he could move like a hummingbird when he was spun up about something. All that fluttering was hard to negotiate from the height of a wheelchair but Bob managed to avoid a collision.

'Thank God you're finally here,' cried Sam. He was pink-cheeked and breathless. 'Something's going on with my computer.'

'Again? I thought Karen sent a tech up here yesterday.' Bob pulled his cell phone from his jacket pocket, frustrated he had to do everything himself. He was the CIO for Christ's sake, not the butler. 'Let me give her a call and see if I can't have her send someone up.'

'She did send someone. Third time this week. The useless son of a bitch said he couldn't find anything wrong with it.' Sam retreated to his desk, motioning for Bob to follow. His suspenders pulled taut and the buttons of his blue pinstripe shirt strained against the movement of his body as he climbed into his chair. 'It's all that damn woman's fault. Can't get a lick of good help around here since she took over IT.'

Bob wondered if Karen Forrester's ears were burning as he pocketed his phone and wheeled around to Sam's side of the desk. 'Well, I've been known to fix a computer or two in my day. What's the problem?'

'I'll tell you what the problem is,' said Sam, pointing to his computer display. 'The problem is the damn thing's possessed.' He slid out of his chair and walked over to where a water carafe was sitting on the credenza. 'It happened again! Not even an hour ago, I was over here pouring myself a glass of water when, out of the corner of my eye, I could see the damn mouse moving. It was moving like someone had their hand on it but that can't be because I was over here.'

Bob cleared his throat. 'So, ah, did you see the actual device moving or just the cursor?'

Sam blinked. 'The cursor, of course. Isn't that what I just said?'

'And the technician checked everything out and said it was fine?'

'Yes, goddamn it, but he's wrong.' Sam heaved himself back into his chair. 'I know what I saw, Bob. I even ran over here and grabbed hold of it just to see if I could make it stop.'

'What happened when you did that?'

'Wouldn't let me do a damn thing. Seemed like the whole computer was frozen solid.' He glared at the computer sitting on the floor under his desk and gave it a kick. 'You know, I used to get twice as much done when all I had was a telephone and a typewriter.' He looked at Bob. 'I called Karen straight away but everything was back to normal by the time that little piss-ant tech showed up. He didn't believe me, as usual, so I called you.'

Bob looked at Sam's computer screen. The cursor sat motionless, waiting. He turned to look at Sam. 'It could just be mouse drift. Maybe if you would give up the trackball mouse—'

'There's nothing wrong with that mouse. It's ergonomic and it was expensive. It stays.' Sam slid out of his chair again, frustrated.

'When is that consultant supposed to get here?'

'This afternoon.'

'Good. I want you to send her up as soon as she's settled.'

'She's going to have a lot on her plate when she gets here, Sam. It could be a few weeks.' And it would be weeks, if he had anything to say about it. He needed Dana to stay focused.

'Nonsense. Have her up here tomorrow.' Sam looked out his window at the yellowing fields dotted with trees and brush as far as the eye could see. 'I hope to hell she's as good as you say. We need all the help we can get after what happened to the last one.'

Dana swore. According to her GPS, it would take another twenty minutes in traffic to get to Grasslands Energy Solutions and it was already a quarter till. She needed to go faster. The engine of her '98 Chevy Lumina strained against the drag of the air conditioner. There hadn't been time to let the A/C run—the best she could do was turn it up to max and open the back windows to let the hot air out. She felt a bead of sweat trail down her lower back. It was officially the best day ever.

How could Floretta do this to her? How could Bob, for that matter? Four years without so much as a glimpse across a room and now she's supposed to just waltz in all professional-like and act like everything is normal? Fat chance of that.

To make matters worse, the dossier on GES was sparse. All she knew was that they specialized in oil and gas extraction technology and energy management software. Whatever that meant.

The company's headquarters was located in a business park

near the edge of the city. Her shirt was completely stuck to her back by the time she pulled in. A delicious blast of cold air swept over her as she crossed the threshold of the plain, square building but there was no time to enjoy it. She was late and the assistant waiting for her at the entrance made sure she knew it.

Her punishment was a cramped, windowless conference room with no cell signal. The small space was overwhelmed by a rectangular oak table. Even the walls were crowded, with mostly-outdated glossy posters of oil derricks and assorted geological maps lining every available surface. A fake ficus, frosted with dust, was wedged indecorously into a corner. She pulled out her phone. Dead zone or not, there was always Angry Birds.

She was still smashing Bad Piggies when a familiar voice called from the doorway, startling her.

'Hello Dana.'

Even in a wheelchair, Bob filled the doorway and then some. Before the accident, he stood over six feet tall. Strangely, he didn't seem much shorter seated. There was a touch more gray in his dark hair than when she last saw him but he still had the same lopsided grin and his eyes, a bright lapis blue, still reminded her of a mischievous boy. Sitting there in his usual trousers and matching suit vest, she could almost imagine him as his old self again—almost.

She put her phone away and got right to the point. 'Why am I here?'

'It's good to see you, too,' he replied, his faint Kentucky drawl edged with sarcasm.

'Is it?'

Bob's body was relaxed but his eyes shone with an expression she knew all too well. He didn't like this any more than she did.

'You're not gonna make this easy on me, are you?' he asked, easing his way into the room. 'Glad to see some things haven't changed.'

'Did you really bring me here to reminisce? I seem to recall we didn't like each other very much the last time we spoke.' She dared him to take the bait. He didn't.

'I brought you here because I need someone I can trust.'

'Someone you can trust?' She almost laughed. 'That's rich, coming from you.' She didn't bother to hide her derision. 'And what makes you think you can trust me after our last encounter?'

He shrugged. 'That was personal. This is business.'

'Then why make it personal by dragging me in here?' She pulled herself to her feet and stuffed her notebook into her bag. 'Call Floretta and tell her you want someone else.'

'I don't need to call Floretta—she called me. For some reason, she wasn't sure you'd show.' He wheeled closer, forcing her to look at him. 'You wouldn't be here if you were serious about resigning so my guess is you're at least curious about what's going on here.'

Dana didn't answer. She couldn't answer. She hadn't been in the same room with this man in years and she didn't know what she thought about any of it.

He took her hesitation as a sign of interest. 'There have been incidents,' he continued. 'Mostly minor but enough that we could see a trend developing. I handed the investigation off to Bennie a while back.'

Dana recognized the name. 'Bennie? Bennie Price? Didn't he work for you when you were at BDS?'

'He did. I took him with me when I came here. Probably one of the best decisions I ever made. He was the only loyal employee I had for the entire first year. We were a good team, too. Or at least we were until Karen showed up and threw a wrench in the works.'

'Who's Karen?'

Bob grimaced. 'Karen Forrester, the IT director. Been here about eighteen months. She wasn't my first pick for the job but the board wasn't especially interested in my opinion at the time.'

'I don't understand. Doesn't the IT director work for you?'

'Not when she's the daughter of the chairman of the board.'

Dana's eyebrows flew up at that. It wasn't the answer she expected but it was an answer. 'So I take it, then, that she doesn't share your, uh, vision?'

'Let's just say she doesn't cotton to people interfering with her department or with her employees, no matter who they are.'

'Vainglorious or megalomaniacal?'

Bob cracked a smile. 'Yes.' His smile abruptly faded. 'Bennie was technically her employee so she took over directing his activities, effectively halting the work I started.'

'So how did you manage to get him to report to you on this investigation?'

'I called it a special project. I have a good relationship with the president of the company, Sam Porter, and he backed me up.'

'So am I assisting Bennie here or am I taking over?'

'Taking over. Both the investigation and his regular job.'

'So how is it that Bennie was loyal enough to leave BDS for you but now you're looking for someone to do his job?'

Bob shifted in his chair and looked away. 'Because he's dead.'

Dana was aghast. 'Are you serious?'

'I wish I wasn't.'

'When?' she sputtered, still processing the news. 'How?'

'A little over a week ago. As for the how, the unofficial report is that he committed suicide.'

Dana was stunned. She seemed to recall that Bennie was a little high-strung but it was difficult to imagine him harming himself. 'If that's the unofficial report, what's the official version?'

'Undetermined,' replied Bob. 'Based on the evidence, the coroner can't rule out the possibility of homicide. The cops are investigating.'

'How can you possibly know anything about an open police investigation?'

'I have a friend in the OKCPD. She can't give me details, of course, but she knows why I'm interested so she shares what she can.'

'And why are you interested?'

Bob leaned forward and lowered his voice. 'Bennie tried to arrange a meeting with me just before he died. He said he found something, something big.'

'And then, rather conveniently, he offed himself before he could make it to that meeting,' she finished.

'Exactly.'

'It makes sense that you would be suspicious under the circumstances but it's hardly conclusive. What did your lady friend, the cop, have to say about it?'

Bob flashed his characteristic grin. '*Lady friend?* Careful there, Sorensen, or I might start to think you're jealous.' He straightened in his chair. 'She didn't say much of anything, but then what could she say? Like you said, it's not exactly a smoking gun.'

'So you think whatever happened to Bennie happened as a result of something he found during his investigation here at GES?'

'Yes.'

'And your first instinct was *not* to hand the whole thing over to the authorities but, instead, to resume that same investigation yourself?'

'Yes.'

She whistled. 'Well, I guess that explains why you asked for me. No sense in throwing someone you actually care about into the line of fire.'

Bob swore. 'Don't be a baby. It's not like that and you know it.'

'How is it not like that?'

'Bennie didn't know to be careful. You do. And I'll be with you every step of the way to keep you safe.'

'I seem to recall you making a similar promise to me before, a promise you didn't keep.'

Bob wheeled away from her, suddenly agitated. 'You don't get to do that. You don't get to throw that in my face, not now.'

It wasn't the right time or place but she couldn't bring herself to drop it. 'Why not? It's not like we ever really talked about it.'

'And we're sure as hell not gonna talk about it now,' he spat, eyes flashing. 'You weren't there. Whatever happened, however it happened, it happened to me.'

'It happened to both of us.'

'Yeah, well, if that's the case then I sure got the short end of the stick.'

She clamped her eyes shut and took a deep breath, willing herself to hold it together. Bob never did know how to deal with a crying woman—he didn't know how to cry himself. It didn't matter, she decided. None of it mattered. He was right. She was wrong to dredge up the past. It was well past time to move on as it was.

She forced herself to change the subject. 'Did he give any indication of what he was on to?'

'No.'

'Did you find anything on his computer?'

'No.'

'Did he leave any notes behind?'

'Just the one where he said he was done living, if we are to believe he actually wrote it.'

She found the edge of the table and leaned on it, reaching up to massage her temples. She avoided Bob's gaze. 'You know as well as I do it's impossible to know everything there is to know about even the most basic network. You're talking about a needle in a haystack here.'

'All I'm asking is that you give it your best shot.'

'You're asking for a miracle.'

'The answers are there if you know where to look,' he persisted.

Her head snapped up. 'Sure they are, if somebody remembered to press the record button. Digital evidence isn't limited to hard drives, you know.'

'Listen—.'

'No, *you* listen. We're not talking about a situation where I can just walk in and ask your staff to lay the network bare for my scrutiny—we're talking about me going undercover in your company to sniff out a possible crime. A possible crime that may or may not have led to the demise of one of your employees. I'm an outsider, Bob. I will have restricted access at best. 'Easy' and 'straightforward' are not concepts that apply here.'

She felt for the gold chain at her neck, mostly concealed by her shirt, and fiddled with the ring beneath the fabric, dangling from the end like a pendant. Once upon a time, it had been an engagement ring but, in recent years, it was the thing she couldn't let go of. She had half a mind to lift it from around her neck and throw it at him right there but then he'd know she still had it, that she was still wearing it. She wouldn't give him the satisfaction. She gathered up her bag before trying to step around him.

Bob grabbed her arm before she could pass. 'You're not getting rid of me so easily. We have a job to do, you and I.' He released her arm. 'We need to work together.'

'I do my best work alone. You should know that better than

anyone.' She took a deep breath before continuing. 'I'll send you status reports via email.'

He shook his head. 'It's too risky. We have to assume that all normal communications inside the building are compromised. I'll send a text to your personal number with a meeting place. Somewhere away from here.'

She couldn't manage anything more than a stiff nod as she stepped around him and headed for the door. He stopped her just as she was about to exit.

'Look,' he said as he came up behind her, 'I know how hard this is for you, for both of us. Just do this one thing for me and you'll never have to see me again. As soon as you figure out what he found, I'll cut you loose.'

She turned to face him. 'What if Bennie did kill himself?' she ventured. 'Have you even considered that? Sometimes it happens without warning, without explanation. What if he just finally decided he'd had enough, that there wasn't anything left worth holding on for?'

Bob fell silent, his expression unreadable. 'No,' he said at last, 'I would've known. He couldn't hide something like that from me.'

Dana looked a him for a long moment. Whatever else was going on in his head, he believed what he was saying. 'Fine,' she said. 'It's your money—if you want to play spy games, then let's play. Just remember, all that glitters is not gold. If it's in the ground, I'll dig it up but you might not like what I find.'

The GES IT department occupied a large space on the first

floor of the building. Employee desks were situated in drab gray, half-walled cubicles in the center of the room. The handful of offices that lined the exterior walls were presumably reserved for supervisors, although none seemed to be present. In fact, hardly anyone was around. A petite, blonde-headed woman sitting at a nearby cubicle noticed her and smiled.

'Can I help you?' she asked. She had a small, soft voice that matched her dainty features. Dana couldn't help but wonder what this woman did for GES. In her perfectly coordinated pale green skirt and sweater set, she looked more like a Kindergarten teacher than a system administrator.

'Yes, thank you,' replied Dana. 'Do you happen to know where I can find Karen Forrester?'

The small woman's eyes widened. 'Oh! You're the consultant!' Her voice dropped to a near whisper. 'They told us you were coming. You're here to take over for Bennie.'

'I think it's more accurate to say I'm here to help. I actually used to know Bennie, although I didn't know him very well. I wish I were here under different circumstances.'

The woman smiled softly. 'Me, too. My name is Ruby by the way. I'll go tell Karen you're here.'

Ruby walked over to the large corner office and knocked before opening the door to stick her head in. Moments later, Karen Forrester stepped out. The IT director was striking in her sleek skirt suit and stiletto heels. Her platinum blonde hair was swept into an immaculate updo that rivaled any magazine cover Dana had ever seen. She looked more like a femme fatale than the controlling woman described by Bob.

Karen assessed her with a critical eye as she approached. 'Well, if it isn't our special guest.' She spoke with a pleasing Texas drawl that didn't quite seem to match the rest of her. 'I was beginning to wonder what became of you.'

'I was in a meeting with Bob. He was telling me about the current situation here,' Dana explained, glancing at her watch. 'I guess it lasted longer than I realized.'

'Bob? I didn't realize the two of you knew each other.'

Dana sensed Karen had more than a passing interest. 'We used to work for the same company, although that was years ago now.'

'How nice that you should remain friends.'

'More like acquaintances.'

'I see,' replied Karen. Dana thought she perceived a tiny shift in Karen's voice. Was it relief?

'Well, more like acquaintances or not,' continued Karen, 'I have to ask that you refer to the CIO as Mr. Leroy while you're here. Although you're not a GES employee, per se, I'm sure you can appreciate that we have a certain way of doing things around here.'

It was tempting to play the he-and-I-used-to-be-engaged-and-have-sex-all-the-time card just to watch the other woman's head explode but she refrained. If Bob was right and there was something nefarious going on at GES, broadcasting their connection would only serve to undermine their efforts. She would just have to suck it up.

'I understand,' Dana replied with as much sincerity as she

could muster. 'I'll just call him Bob in private.'

Karen's expression wavered slightly but she didn't acknowledge the comment. Clearly, she was a woman who knew how to pick her battles. 'Well, then, now that we have that out of the way, why don't I show you to your office?' She motioned for Dana to follow as she led the way. 'I was planning to put you up in the conference room but I think I'll just put you in Bennie's old office instead so you can have some privacy.' She paused to look back at Dana. 'That won't be a problem, will it?'

Dana knew a dare when she heard one. 'Not at all,' she assured the IT director. She could handle a dead guy's office—maybe.

Karen halted only briefly at the sight of Bennie's personal belongings still scattered around the room. As they say, time and tide wait for no man and Karen was no exception. Whatever she once thought of her employee, she was clearly over the loss. She smoothed the front of her skirt as her eyes swept around the room.

'I'll send Ruby in with a box to clear these things out of your way,' she said, picking up Bennie's jacket—still slung over the back of his chair—and draping it over her arm. 'She'll also bring you a key card and get you set up on the computer. She's your assistant while you're here so let her know if there's anything else you need.' She turned to leave but stopped at the door. 'Also, I want a daily activity report—email is fine—and I have to ask that you don't go wandering around the building without an escort. I'm sure you understand.'

Karen didn't wait for a reply. She simply vanished through the door without another word.

Alone again, Dana surveyed her new surroundings. An L-shaped desk and a matching bookcase and filing cabinet filled the space. The oak veneer looked cheap. Laminate, probably. There was also a narrow window framed with vertical blinds, a single straight-backed chair that looked like it had never been sat in, and, of course, Bennie's chair. The thought of sitting in it made her shiver.

His personal items included a pencil holder made of old 3.5-inch floppy disks and zip ties—filled with actual pencils, though mostly dulled—and an impressive selection of action figures. Some vintage, some newer, but all well-cared for. An oversized poster of Captain America, his patriotic colors blazing bright, rounded out the collection.

She tested the center desk drawer to see if it would open and found a couple of Transformers mixed in with the office supplies. She couldn't help but smile. Not a single villain in the bunch. Bennie must have been an optimist.

She finally took the plunge and sat down at his desk, in his chair. It was oddly intimate. She tweaked a bobble head doll perched at the base of the computer display and stared past her own reflection into the blackness of the screen. What was the *something big* that sent Bennie scuttling off to Bob? Did it really lead to his death? She shook her head. It was simply too much to believe. Yet here she was. She spun in the chair. How ironic that Bob would ask her to recreate Bennie's last steps. If the man was doing his job right, there would be no footprints to find.

CHAPTER TWO

Mayhem and Intrigue—or Ghosts

The large oak stood tall in the early morning light, bracing itself for another dog-day of summer. Dana pointed the hose at it, splashing water at its base in hopes of revitalizing its drooping leaves while keeping herself as dry as possible. She laughed at her own efforts. In this drought, a few gallons of water was about as good as a single drop. The only thing getting properly soaked were her shoes.

The cicadas were singing a drowsy chorus in the trees, occasionally joined by the trill of a cricket, while the birds called each other from the branches. They were probably discussing the squirrels, who were already up and about, pilfering heavily from the squirrel-proof bird feeders.

She caught a whiff of honeysuckle and mint, carried by a breeze barely strong enough to make the wind chimes sway. The scent reminded her of the countless summer days she spent here as a child, running through the sprinkler and eating sun-warmed watermelon out on the front porch while her Aunt Tillie, who wasn't really her aunt, battled the meddlesome plants that were forever cropping up in unwanted places. Now it was Dana's turn to hunt down the invasive vines and shoots and dig them out of the ground. But not today. Today, she would just enjoy their sweet fragrance.

A plume of white dust appeared at the end of the driveway and soon gave way to the sound of tires crunching on gravel. It was Mazie, right on time as usual. Dana turned the water off and flopped the hose into the shade before walking out to greet her. Mazie parked under a tree, chasing off a flock of grasshoppers in the process, and leapt out of her SUV, smiling and wind-blown, with a plate of biscuits in her hands.

'You'll *never guess* who I just saw turning into old Mrs. Smalley's place,' she said as she tried to negotiate the shifting gravel in her modest gray heels.

'Who?'

'*Mary Marie Bridenstine.*'

'Mary Marie Bridenstine? As in Jake Bridenstine's daughter, the one you hate? I haven't seen her in years. How'd she look?'

Mazie's smile broadened. 'Terrible,' she said, handing Dana the plate of biscuits. They were still warm. 'Bleach-bottle blonde, years of tanning gone awry, and, best of all, fatter than me.'

Dana laughed as she led the way into the house. 'Well, so long as you're happy about it.'

'After she teased me for being fat all through high school?' replied Mazie, following her into the kitchen. 'Hell, yes, I'm happy about it. Well, mostly happy—you know how I hate to see a big lady out in the wild with hardly nothin' on. It's a disgrace to the uniform.'

Dana put the biscuits down on the kitchen table. 'How much nothing are we talking about?'

'Well, I just saw the top of her but that was plenty. That strappy little tank top she was wearing didn't cover much. Big ol' floppy boobs hanging down—lumps, bumps, stubbly pits, stretch marks... shoot, if I wanted to see all that, I could just go home and stand naked in front of a mirror.'

'Maybe it's just her way of showing men that there's plenty of her to hold on to,' suggested Dana, forcing herself to stop laughing long enough to put on a pot of coffee and pull a jar of strawberry rhubarb jam out of the fridge.

Mazie was skeptical. 'What, so they won't fall off?'

'Well, a man's gotta stay in the saddle somehow, right?'

Mazie split one of the biscuits with a butter knife and reached for the jam. 'Even so, if somebody wants to shove their boobs in my face, they should be nice looking boobs.'

'So I guess that means my boobs are out.'

'Hell, yes,' said Mazie between bites. 'If you let them things loose, they're liable to smother somebody to death. Why do you think I never try to hug you?'

'I'll have you know there are plenty of men who have fantasized about what they can do with my cleavage, thank you very much,' jested Dana, setting two empty coffee mugs on the table.

Mazie snorted. 'Like that guy who's always checking you out at work? The one up on the fourth floor?'

'Ben?' Dana chuckled at the thought. '*That* will never happen. He's way too small for my cleavage. He'd never make it out alive.' She looked at her watch. 'Shit. I have to leave for work in twenty minutes.'

Mazie got up and poured them both a cup of coffee. 'Speaking of work, how did it go yesterday?'

'If by *it*, you mean Bob, then it went fine. Sort of.'

'Sort of?'

'Well, you may as well know. He wants me to catch a murderer.'

Mazie choked on her coffee. 'I beg your pardon?'

'Yup. He's convinced the last security analyst was killed on account of something he discovered at the company, if you can believe that, and he conveniently died before anyone knew what that was.' Dana took a swig of her coffee before continuing. 'Bob is convinced I can figure it out.'

'That's the dumbest thing I've ever heard! He can't just call in a consultant to do the job of the police. Can he? Are you actually going along with this?'

Dana set her coffee mug on the table. 'Do you remember Bennie Price?'

'Sure. Used to work for Bob, right?'

'That's the one. And it turns out he's the one who died. The cause of his death is apparently undetermined.'

Mazie's eyes widened in disbelief. 'No way! Bennie Price is dead?' She fell silent for a minute, digesting the news before continuing. 'He was from around here, you know. I think my mom knows the family. Do you think it's really possible that someone killed him?'

Dana grabbed a biscuit off the plate. 'Your guess is as good as mine. I was in his office until seven o'clock last night trying to find something—anything—that might tell me what he was working on.'

'Nothing?'

'Not so far. It was just a first pass but I'm not holding my breath.'

'Is it possible someone destroyed the evidence, so to speak?'

'I suppose we can't rule it out, but, if someone did go through his stuff, they were careful. It would've taken time. Uninterrupted access to his office, to his computer.' Dana rubbed her eyes and groaned. 'So much about this whole situation just doesn't make any sense.'

Mazie sat back in her chair and thought about that. 'Maybe Bennie was the one being careful,' she said at last. 'What did Bob have to say about it?'

'He didn't. As a matter of fact, for someone so convinced a crime has been committed, he's awfully short on theories.'

'You think he's not telling you everything?'

'I wouldn't put it past him. Honestly, I don't know what to think.'

'So, uh, how is he?'

'Bob? He's fine, I guess.'

'How does he look?'

Dana grimaced. She'd heard that tone before, more times than she could count. 'Are you asking about his health or are you asking if I still find him attractive?'

Mazie grinned. 'I'm just asking how he looks.'

'He looks good,' said Dana, feeling her cheeks turn warm. Better than good, if she was being honest with herself. Yet another complication she didn't need. She stood and started clearing the dishes, pretending not to notice Mazie's smug expression. She couldn't allow herself the distraction of swooning over a pair of blue eyes when her career was on the line. And as much as he claimed to trust her, she didn't trust him any further than she could throw him, chair and all.

Her thoughts were interrupted by the sound of another vehicle crunching up the drive. She lifted a corner of the pale yellow curtain covering the bottom half of the window over the sink and spotted the silhouette of a dark sedan through the gravel dust.

Mazie crowded up beside her to look over her shoulder. 'Are you expecting someone?'

'No,' replied Dana, squinting to make out the driver. 'It's probably my father, coming around to try and make peace again. He's been showing up at odd hours lately.'

The sedan came to a stop in front of the house. The dust settled and a stranger stepped out. There was something glinting on his belt.

Mazie whistled. 'Damn. Is that a badge?'

Dana could feel Mazie pressed against her back, angling for a closer look. The stranger looked to be in his mid-fifties, quite slender and not much taller than her own 5-foot-3 frame. He was well dressed in a gray suit with a clean, white shirt and an understated tie. Whoever this man was, he was no ordinary cop.

She dropped the curtain before he had a chance to catch her watching him and motioned for Mazie to tidy up while she headed for the front door, smoothing her hair as she went.

The stranger was holding the screen door wide, preparing to knock, just as she opened the door to the house. The rush of warm air mingling with cool air from inside surprised them both.

'I apologize for disturbing you at this hour, ma'am,' he began, holding out his credentials. 'My name is Detective Richard Mercer. I'm with the OKCPD and I was hoping you might have a few minutes this morning to chat with me.'

Dana looked at the badge and ID in his outstretched hand. She studied both briefly before waving him inside. She wouldn't recognize a counterfeit if she saw one but the photo was definitely a match. She couldn't decide if he was younger than he looked or older but he had a nice face and a pleasant voice. Not harmless, perhaps, but certainly not threatening.

'Of course, come on in.' She gestured to the kitchen. 'As it happens, you're not my first guest today. My friend and I were just having coffee and biscuits. Would you care to join us?'

Hearing herself mentioned, Mazie stuck her head through the doorway. She looked at the newcomer with interest and gave him a smile but remained silent, shock of all shocks.

If Detective Mercer was surprised by the turn of events, he

didn't let on. 'I could do with a cup of coffee, thank you. But I was hoping we could talk in private.' He looked at Mazie. 'Police business, I hope you understand.'

Mazie smiled sweetly. 'As a matter of fact, I do understand. Which is why I think I'll just go ahead and take myself off to work.' She swept up her purse and sailed out the front door, coffee cup still in hand. She motioned for Dana to call her later as she let the screen door slam shut behind her and disappeared from view.

Dana led Detective Mercer into the kitchen and poured them both a cup of coffee before settling down in the chair opposite him.

'You're probably wondering why I'm here,' he ventured.

'I have an inkling.'

His eyes widened somewhat. 'Oh?'

'Well, it's not everyday a girl gets the call to unearth the motive behind a man's murder. It sort of stands out. And now I have a detective at my door. It's not a big leap.'

Detective Mercer set his coffee down and leaned in. 'Are you telling me a man's been murdered?'

Dana leaned forward in kind. 'Are you?'

He chuckled and shook his head. She had the feeling she'd just impressed him somehow.

'To be honest, I was hoping you could tell me,' he said.

'Well now we're just going in circles.' She poured a little more milk into her coffee to cool it off before continuing. 'Look, I can appreciate your coming here to see what I know but the truth is I don't know anything. In fact, I'm more than a little skeptical about the whole thing myself. I know Bob Leroy is convinced Bennie was the victim of foul play, and, hell, maybe he was, but I spent several hours alone in his office last night and came up empty. Whatever you're looking for, it's probably not there.'

Detective Mercer nodded. 'I was afraid of that. Have you discussed any of this with Mr. Leroy?'

She shrugged. 'Yes and no. Why? Haven't you already spoken to him?'

'No. He's actually been speaking to one of my colleagues in another unit. She's the one who told me about your involvement. She thought you might have some useful insight.'

'Sorry to disappoint you.'

He pulled a business card from the inside pocket of his jacket and laid it on the table. 'You didn't. Quite the contrary, in fact. It's good that you're skeptical.' He stood and pointed to the card. 'If you do happen to find anything of interest, I'd appreciate it if you'd give me a call. I'd also appreciate it if you'd keep this between you and me for the time being,' he added. 'It's hard to know who to trust in a case like this so it's usually better not to trust anyone at all.'

Detective Mercer thanked her again for the coffee before disappearing down the drive exactly the way he came in. Dana glanced at the time on her phone. Karen was probably passed out with rage by now. What a shame she couldn't be there to see it.

She picked up the business card and tossed it in the junk drawer before making sure the coffee pot was turned off. She set the window units to 85 degrees and finally headed out to the metal shed where she parked her car. It wasn't until she reached the main road that it occurred to her. Detective Mercer never actually said Bennie Price was murdered but he also never said he wasn't.

After three failed attempts to read the same paragraph, Bob tossed his reading glasses on his desk in disgust and vigorously rubbed at his temples. Another migraine. He'd been swallowing pills all morning and nothing would touch it, not even his prescription meds. It didn't help knowing that Dana was somewhere in the building, doing lord knows what. She was probably burning the entire program to the ground just to sift through the ashes. He knew her too well to believe otherwise. It was a risk he'd just have to take. He needed answers.

The phone rang. It was Helen, his assistant. 'Ms. Forrester is here to see you. Can I send her in?'

He swore. A visit from Karen was just what he needed. 'Fine, but call me in ten minutes.' He wanted a good excuse to throw her out.

Moments later, she strode in. She didn't bother with formalities. 'We need to talk about your consultant friend,' she said, coming to a halt in front of his desk.

'What about her?' He gestured to one of the chairs in front of his desk, hoping she'd prefer to stand. She didn't.

'I want you to get rid of her,' said Karen, taking a seat and turning her body to give him the best possible view of her toned legs.

'Why would I want to do that? She just got here.'

'Let's just say she doesn't take instruction well. Besides, she's not a GES employee—there's no reason for her to be poking around where she doesn't belong.'

'You're right, she's not a GES employee. She's a consultant who's been given a job to do and she's doing it. Like it or not, we need a security analyst and I'm not about to throw some chump in the seat just so you can avoid an unpleasant encounter.'

'She's an outsider.'

'She's trustworthy, you have my word on that. And if that's not good enough, then just try to remember that she works for one of the most reputable information security firms in the country. She's spent the better part of fifteen years working in the field—she knows what she's doing.'

Karen searched his face. 'You seem to know her pretty well.'

'I should, I used to work with her.' Among other things.

'So she said. Still, though, I can't help but wonder if there isn't more to it.' She shifted in the chair so that her skirt inched higher. 'How do you suppose she would react if she knew about us?'

Bob leaned forward in his chair. 'There is no us.'

Karen's eyes widened in feigned surprise. 'What, have you already forgotten our little tryst?'

'Once. We were together once. And that was a year ago.' He took a deep breath and tried to ignore the pounding in his head. 'It was a mistake,' he said at last. 'And you know it.'

Karen smiled coyly. 'Maybe, but I'm still willing to bet it would ruffle the feathers of your old *acquaintance* if I let that little tidbit slip.'

'Do whatever you want,' he snapped. 'Knock yourself out. Just don't come running to me when she puts you in your place.'

'Oh, please, I'd like to see her try. Besides, she'll be gone before it ever comes to that.'

'What makes you so sure of that?'

She shrugged. 'She's only here until I hire a replacement. And, as it happens, I just came from HR and they've agreed to make this position a priority.' She studied her manicure before continuing. 'The job advertisement should be posted by the end of the day. So the way I see it, Ms. Sorensen won't be here long enough to make it worth her while so you may as well send her back.'

'It'll take weeks to get a decent applicant pool, maybe months.'

'I don't think so,' she replied smugly. 'I happen to know a few people who are already interested. In fact, I expect to see resumes start coming in by the end of the week.'

'And are these people qualified?'

'By your standards? Probably not. But let's face it, Bob, we don't have a requirement for someone of Ms. Sorensen's caliber. We can't afford it. And, I might add, we never had it in the first place. Even you have to admit Bennie couldn't compete with someone like her.'

'Bennie had more technical ability than you give him credit for. He was underutilized.'

'All the more reason to hire someone with more administrative experience. A technical background would be wasted here.'

'Not if the job is done right.'

The phone rang. Bob snatched it up, frustrated. It was Helen, sweet Helen, throwing him a life preserver. He glanced at the time. Bless her, she called one minute early. Hanging up the phone, he looked at Karen with as much regret as he could manage. 'I'm sorry, I have to cut this short. I have another meeting. But we're not done with this discussion—not by a long shot.'

'If you say so. Maybe we could talk about it over dinner?' She laughed at the expression on his face and rose from her seat to leave. 'Well, if you change your mind, you know where to find me.' When she reached the door, she called back, 'By the way, you really shouldn't bother lying. You're no good at it. I know you don't have another meeting.' She laughed again, enjoying her own cleverness, and winked at him before finally disappearing through the doorway.

Bob swore and closed his eyes, willing the throbbing in his head to subside. When Dana found out about him and Karen, she'd probably march into his office and stab him in the heart. Or at least he hoped she would. He pushed the thought aside. He couldn't afford the luxury of dwelling on personal matters with Karen on the offensive. He was running out of time.

He reached into his pocket for his key ring and unlocked the file drawer in his desk. He pulled out a rubber-banded bundle of notebooks and papers sandwiched around a thumb drive. Getting them out of Bennie's office hadn't been easy but he couldn't risk leaving them behind for someone to find. He rubbed at his temples again. As much as he'd hoped to avoid involving Dana in this mess, he may not have a choice. He sighed. He'd just have to cross that bridge when he came to it. In the meantime, Karen wasn't the only one who could influence HR.

He reached for the phone. He was still the CIO of this outfit—he might not be able to stop her but he could sure as hell slow her down.

Dana shoved the last piece of paper in the stack away from her and dropped her head into her hands. It was almost lunchtime and she still hadn't made any progress. She looked up at the bare shelves and wondered if she'd missed something and shook her head. She couldn't have.

She leaned her head back in the chair and stared at the ceiling, retracing everything she'd done so far. She and Ruby had spent the morning packing Bennie's belongings into boxes and cleaning the place from top to bottom. Everything work-related was organized into piles and she'd just finished going through the last one. The computer was clean. Even the documents stored on the file server proved to be of little interest.

The only thing out of place were the pencils. Dozens of pencils, not so much as a single sheet of blank paper to write on. So why were most of the pencils dull? It was the damnedest thing. She sighed. Whatever she was looking for, she wasn't going to find it in here.

There was a knock at the door. She turned her head to see Ruby standing there with a concerned look on her face.

'Is this a bad time?'

'Oh, don't mind me,' said Dana, sitting up in the chair like a normal person. 'I was just thinking. Blank surfaces help me focus.

Ceilings, especially.'

'I was just wondering if there was anything you needed,' said Ruby, somewhat haltingly. Dana wondered if she'd been sent to check up on her.

'As a matter of fact, I could use a little help.' She stepped around the desk to unload a pile of documents from the small, straight-backed chair and cleared a path for Ruby to sit down. 'You might be able to help me understand a few things.'

Ruby blushed. 'I'll help if I can but you probably want to talk to someone who knows a lot more than I do.'

Dana smiled. 'Well, first off, you and I were never properly introduced. I have no idea what you do here. I don't even know your last name.'

Ruby's blush deepened as she smiled. 'I mostly help out with the phones. I also monitor the help desk trouble ticket system and compile reports for Karen. And I'm usually the one to set up network accounts and user permissions for new employees. Make sure they understand the rules, that sort of thing. Nothing really special.'

'It sounds like they keep you pretty busy all the same. Do you ever help out with the more technical stuff?'

Ruby perked up. 'I used to do a lot of that when I was taking classes at the vo-tech. I wanted to be a system administrator.' The slightly wistful expression on her face faded. 'I don't really get to do anything like that here, though.'

'Did you work with Bennie much?'

'Not really. We would occasionally talk about what he was

working on but, for the most part, we talked about other things.'

'So were the two of you friends?'

Dana didn't think it was possible, but Ruby blushed even more.

'At the office, mostly. Sometimes we'd get together after work but we hadn't done that in a long while.'

'I'm sorry for your loss. I know how much it hurts to lose someone you care about.'

Ruby looked down at her hands, folded neatly in her lap. 'I keep reminding myself that he's with his Lord now, smiling down on all of us, but it's hard.' She looked up again and smiled. 'I think he'd be glad to know you're here, looking out for things. His job was always important to him.'

'I'm glad you said that because I do have a few questions about some of what I've been looking at,' replied Dana. She rifled through one of the piles and pulled out a document. 'For example, there's an incident response plan here but it appears to be outdated. Do you know if there's a more recent version?'

Ruby took the document from her and studied it. 'I'm sorry, this is the only version I know of.'

'I was afraid of that.'

'I don't understand. Is the date really that important?'

'It's not the date, it's the plan itself,' said Dana, holding up the document. 'It won't work. And that means it's not actually being implemented.' Seeing Ruby's puzzled expression, she continued. 'It describes how incidents *should* be handled, not how they *will* be handled. Contrary to popular belief, there is a difference. Minus any sort of practical implementation, it's just an academic exercise. A means of saying you have a plan without actually having one.' She screwed up her face. 'Well, at least it paints a pretty good picture about how things work around here.'

'How do you mean?'

'A plan like this requires the participation of everyone in the organization, something easier said than done.' Dana shrugged. 'You know how it is—nobody wants to be inconvenienced, nobody wants the extra responsibility. And so you wind up with one guy in an office trying to make something out of nothing.' She looked at the document in her hands. 'It's what happens when the appearance of substance is more valuable than substance.'

Ruby seemed to understand. 'Bennie did tell me a long time ago that things were a real mess when he first got here. I guess he and Mr. Leroy were working to sort it all out but there was a lot to do. They proposed a whole bunch of changes but there were problems. I guess they couldn't convince the CFO to give them the budget they needed.' She looked at her hands. 'Bennie complained about it a lot, actually.'

Dana nodded. 'It's a problem, more common than you might think. It's also not something I can fix while I'm here. It'll just have to wait until the company hires someone full time.' She gestured to the piles of papers stacked around the office. 'I was hoping I could pick up where he left off by looking through all this stuff but there's nothing here I can use. Do you have any idea what he was working on?'

'I know he was busy—he worked late a lot—but I don't know

what he was doing. Maybe Karen knows?'

Dana laughed. 'I'm pretty sure Karen is just tolerating my presence until she can hire someone. I don't expect to get much of anything out of her.'

'You shouldn't take it personally,' Ruby offered. 'She's kind of a hard person to warm up to.'

That was one way to put it. Dana decided to change the subject.

'Bob, or should I say, *Mr. Leroy,* mentioned that Bennie had been looking into a string of incidents here recently. Would any of that be documented in your ticketing system? You know, people calling in because of something unusual going on with their computer?'

'Probably. Would you like me to look?'

'That would be great, but don't bother with it until after lunch. You deserve a break.'

'What about you?'

'Oh, I think I'll just stay a while longer and make sure I didn't miss anything.'

Ruby stood to leave. 'Well, then, I guess I'll see you later.'

Just as she was about to walk out the door, Dana stopped her. 'By the way, you never did tell me what your last name is.'

The blush was back. 'Hornbuckle,' replied Ruby. 'It's kind of a country-sounding name, I know. A lot of people laugh when they hear it.'

Dana chuckled. 'Oh, honey, I've heard way worse than that. Remind me to show you a copy of my family tree some time and we can both have a good laugh.'

Ruby grinned and nodded before finally disappearing out the door. Alone again, Dana picked up the stack of papers closest to her and settled down for another round. Now that she'd seen everything at least once, maybe something would stand out. Or maybe she was just wasting her time. She took a deep breath. She couldn't wait to type up her first status report for Karen. If she was lucky, she'd be fired tomorrow.

Dana sat back on her haunches and surveyed the damage on the floor around her. It was no use. Almost two hours spent pouring over files and all she had to show for it was a mess of scattered papers, a viciously growling stomach, and a general notion that Bennie was basically just doing his job in the weeks leading up to his death. Big whoop. Hopefully Ruby was having more luck with her project.

She was digging a partially crushed package of peanut butter crackers out of her bag when the phone on Bennie's desk rang. She considered ignoring it but it could be Ruby calling to report something interesting. Given the circumstances, she was willing to risk the awkwardness of having to explain Bennie's absence to a total stranger.

'This is Dana,' she answered, hoping she didn't sound like someone who just walked in off the street. She had no idea how they answered their phones around here.

'Yes, hello. This is Sam Porter. I'm ready for you to come up and take a look at my computer.'

'I beg your pardon?' she blurted, more than a little confused. Was she supposed to be a computer technician, too?

There was a pause. 'My computer,' he repeated. 'I'm ready for you to come take a look.'

'I'm sorry, I think you may have dialed the wrong number. I'm not—'

'Aren't you the consultant Bob hired? The one sitting in for Bennie?'

She blinked. 'Yes.'

'You *do* know about computers and networks and all that hooey, right?'

Hooey? Dana cleared her throat. 'I do.'

'Then you're exactly who I meant to call. I'm up on the top floor. Turn left at the elevators, you can't miss it.'

Mr. Porter hung up the phone before she could respond, which was probably just as well since she didn't know what else she could've said anyway. Blowing him off was not an option.

She put the receiver back on the hook and decided it might actually do her some good to get out of the office for a few minutes, even if it did mean getting down on all fours for what would likely turn out to be a loose cable. She pulled her hair back into a low pony tail, slipped into her jacket to make herself look more presentable, and grabbed her bag before making her way to the elevators. She passed a few new faces on her way out but they took no notice of her. Karen's office was dark. She took the latter as a good sign. With any luck, she'd make it back before anyone knew she was gone.

A plump, older woman who introduced herself as Grace sat outside Mr. Porter's office, looking every bit like a modern-day sentinel seated behind an immaculate desk made of solid cherry. Images of starched white shirts and hospital corners sprang to mind as she took in the woman's high-dollar pearls, polished pumps, and tailored houndstooth skirt suit, but she wasn't fooled. Behind the friendly smile was the cunning of a ninja. This lady knew everything that went on at GES and then some, Dana was certain of it.

Grace showed her to a large office where Mr. Porter was perched behind a desk even more impressive than the one she'd just seen.

'You must be Dana Sorensen,' he said warmly, sliding out of his seat to greet her. He came around the desk and reached out to shake her hand. 'Bob has said some mighty good things about you. I trust you didn't have any trouble finding the place?'

'Not at all,' she replied, accepting the handshake. He had a firm grip. 'You were right when you said it was hard to miss.'

Mr. Porter chuckled. 'It'd be a miracle if it were. There's more square footage in this office than there is in my entire house and the view's not even half as nice.' He gestured to the windows and the dry fields beyond. 'This drought is something, ain't it? It's been years since my wife and I came up from San Antone and we're still not used to the weather. Of course, I'm the complainer in the family so I take it harder than she does.' He winked. 'Compared to me, my wife's a saint. Just ask her and she'll tell you.'

Dana grinned. 'So, when you called, you mentioned something

about your computer. Are you having a problem?'

'Didn't Bob tell you?'

'I'm afraid not. At least not yet,' she corrected. 'But, to tell you the truth, he and I really haven't had much of a chance to talk.' She couldn't believe she was racing to Bob's defense but it hardly seemed sportsmanlike to sink his ship on her second day.

'Well, then, let me give you the short version.' Mr. Porter pointed in the direction of his desk. He spoke matter-of-factly. 'My computer is possessed.'

'Possessed?'

'I don't know how else to describe it. Unless, of course, there's such a thing as electrified ghosts.' A look of concern flitted across his face as he considered the possibility. 'There isn't, is there?'

She blinked but managed to keep a straight face. 'Not that I've encountered so far.'

'Oh, don't mind me. My wife watches all them shows on TV about hauntings and such. I think it must be rubbing off on me.' He marched over to the credenza near his desk and poured himself a glass of water. 'It's just that my computer sometimes... *does* things that no one can explain.'

'What kind of things?'

'The mouse moves around on its own. Not to mention the whole damn thing locks up on me at least once a week.' He turned to glower at the space under his desk, presumably where his computer was. 'Sometimes a black box flashes up on the screen and then disappears real quick-like.' He took a swig of his water. 'Other times, I just get the feelin' that I'm not the only one who's been using my computer.'

Well, now, that *was* curious. 'How long has this been going on?'

'Weeks. Hell, by now it's been months.'

'Did Bennie ever look into it?'

'Couple of times, but that was a while back. Those useless sons of bitches downstairs are absolutely no help, either, which is ironic considering they call themselves the *help desk*. All they do is come up here and tell me nothing's wrong.'

Dana pulled out her phone to check the time and saw a handful of unread text messages and a few missed calls, including a recent one from Karen. So much for a clean getaway. It didn't matter, she decided. Mr. Porter might be a little spirited but he wasn't nuts. And she was intrigued. No sense in leaving without at least taking a quick peek under the hood.

Her finger hovered over the glass screen. What were the odds that Karen would allow it? She didn't have to think on it long. She put the phone to sleep and dropped it back into her bag. Sometimes it was just better to ask for forgiveness than to ask for permission.

She turned her attention back to Mr. Porter.

'I can't promise I'll find anything wrong with your system, Mr. Porter, but I'll give it my best shot.'

Mr. Porter eagerly offered his chair so she could begin her work. She had to scramble into it like a child but at least it was high enough to give her comfortable access to the keyboard and mouse. Accessing client systems directly wasn't her preferred method but she didn't have the luxury of time in this case—she'd simply have to be careful.

She didn't bother to inspect the mouse. She could tell just by the way it handled that nothing was mechanically wrong with it. Her first order of business, therefore, was to rule out hardware conflicts.

It was a Windows-based system so she brought up the device manager to see a complete list of installed hardware and found nothing unusual. She wasn't surprised to see that everything, including the mouse, appeared to be functioning properly. Assuming the list actually accounted for everything, that is.

With that in mind, she closed the device manager and switched to the command prompt. The black screen soothed her. Its stark simplicity reminded her that somewhere beneath the sleek interface was a machine. A machine that could be coaxed into revealing its secrets.

'What's that you're doing there?' asked Mr. Porter, eying the DOS screen with suspicion.

'I'm taking a deeper look at your hardware profile,' she answered. 'The screen I was just looking at told me what's currently connected to your computer. If we want to see a complete list of everything that's installed, whether it's connected right now or not, we need to finesse it a little.'

'How will that fix anything?'

'It probably won't,' she replied truthfully. 'But it seems logical to rule out the possibility of a hardware conflict before we go chasing after mayhem and intrigue. Or ghosts.'

'You sound just like Bob,' said Mr. Porter, crossing his arms. 'I don't know how many times I have to repeat myself. There isn't a cotton pickin' thing wrong with that mouse.' He pointed to the screen. 'You go ahead and look in your magic box, it's just gonna tell you I'm right.'

Dana sighed inwardly. Mr. Porter was acting like an expectant father. On the one hand, totally understandable; on the other hand, completely annoying. Fortunately, this was a quick operation—just a matter of setting a variable and starting the device manager console from the command line:

```
C:\Users\porters>set dvmgr_show_nonpresent_devices=1
C:\Users\porters>start devmgmt.msc
```

As expected, Mr. Porter's hardware profile was pretty typical. The only other devices installed on the system were a couple of external USB hard drives and they were definitely not the source of the problem. No mayhem here.

Finally, just to be able to say she did, she ran a quick scan to check for driver conflicts. The results were almost instantaneous. No errors, no conflicts. With just a few clicks of the mouse, she'd hit her first dead end. Mr. Porter was right.

'I tried to tell you,' he said smugly. 'But does anyone ever listen to me? Hell no. So what now?'

She brought the command prompt back up and let herself enjoy the tiny frisson of excitement that raced down her spine. This was the only part of her job she still really enjoyed.

'Now,' she said, 'we look for the thing that doesn't want to be found.'

Technically speaking, the behavior reported by Mr. Porter could be caused by any number of things but there was only one thing of any real concern to her that would cause everything he described at once. The trick would be in figuring it out before Karen came bursting through the door.

A quick review of the installed software yielded nothing of interest but it would be too easy if it did. She was looking for something that had managed to circumvent GES security systems. They may be cheap bastards but the basic countermeasures were in place—infiltrating the system of a senior manager was hardly a cake walk.

She decided to focus on running processes. Malicious code was easy to hide but it still had to run the same as anything else. Perhaps something would pop in the task manager.

The task manager revealed a number of running processes but none stood out as particularly suspicious at first glance. It didn't mean the system was clean, of course, it just meant she'd have to inspect them one by one. And *that* could take hours.

Fortunately, every process was assigned a process identifier—and the PID was a useful little number if you knew what to do with it. And while she didn't have the best tools at her disposal under the circumstances, she could make do.

She closed the task manager and returned to the command prompt. If there was a puppeteer pulling the strings on Mr. Porter's mouse, they would need a reliable way in—and with any luck, they were keeping the door propped open.

Of all the command-line tools she'd used over the years, netstat was easily her favorite. Incoming and outgoing network connections tended to be significant in her line of work. In order for a remote user to access Mr. Porter's machine, there would need to be an application running on his computer capable of establishing that connection. All running applications had at least one associated process and it was those processes that created connections. If the door was open, netstat might just tell her everything she needed to know.

Mr. Porter stirred just as she was about to hit the enter key.

'Netstat -bo,' he read from the screen. 'You computer people sure do have some strange notions.'

She smiled. 'Netstat is the name of a computer program—a utility, really—and the letters signify parameters. This combination of parameters will display the network statistics for your computer that I'm most interested in,' she explained as she hit the enter key.

```
C:\Users\porters>netstat -bo
The requested operation requires elevation.
```

'A combination of parameters that I apparently don't have the authority to run.' She looked at Mr. Porter. 'I don't suppose you would happen to have an account with administrative privileges on this computer?'

'Administrative what?'

'Privileges.' She didn't wait long for an answer. The look on his face was enough. 'No worries,' she said. 'Fortunately for us, there's never just one way to do anything.'

For convenience sake, she re-opened the task manager and adjusted the view so it would display the corresponding PID for each process. Then, returning to the command prompt, she re-entered the original command, making sure to leave off the offending parameter this time around.

She was almost immediately presented with a lengthy list of UDP and TCP connections. Some were ESTABLISHED, several were LISTENING, and a few were hanging out in TIME_WAIT status. Each connection was associated with its corresponding PID; the rest, she would just have to work out manually.

She narrowed her suspect list by comparing each PID identified by netstat to the corresponding PID in the task manager. The ESTABLISHED connections were mostly HTTP connections to the same IP address and were associated with Internet Explorer. No surprises there—most web browsers opened multiple connections in order to fetch web pages faster.

The LISTENING connections were more interesting. She recognized several well-known ports and had no trouble guessing at their function, even before comparing process identifiers, but there was one, in particular, that warranted deeper inspection: PID 2912, no description, associated with *CRE_pt10.exe*, listening on a dynamic port. Was this the thing that didn't want to be found? Maybe, maybe not. But one thing was for certain—it wasn't good.

Mr. Porter tapped her on the shoulder, impatient to hear the verdict. 'I feel like I've been sitting here for a mighty long time, Ms. Sorensen, and I'm ready for some answers. Now are you ready to tell me what you found or are we gonna continue this game of charades?'

Dana swiveled to face him. She knew he wanted answers but

she also knew he wasn't going to like what she had to say. Neither would Bob, for that matter.

'Ghosts, Mr. Porter. I found ghosts.'

CHAPTER THREE

It's a Date

'What do you mean you found ghosts?' Mr. Porter demanded. 'What sort of ghosts?'

Dana spun the chair around to face the computer again and tapped the screen where the name of the executable, *CRE_pt10.exe*, was displayed.

'There's an unknown application on your computer that's listening to the network, waiting for a signal from a remote system to establish a connection. A connection that *could* be making it possible for someone else to gain control of your computer.'

Mr. Porter's brow furrowed as he looked over her shoulder. 'What sort of application? And just how remote are we talking?'

'Well, if it is what I think it is, then we're probably talking about a Trojan of some sort, which is basically just malicious software that makes it's way into a system by hiding inside of something else,' she explained, scooting a little to the side so he could get a better look. 'As for the remote system, technically speaking, it could be anywhere in the world.'

'And just what is it that you think this so-called Trojan is trying to do to my computer?'

She turned to face him again. 'In my experience, there are three basic reasons to attack a system or a network—to take something, to break something, or to prove it's possible. I don't have enough information in front of me right now to say one way or another but, considering the nature of your business and your job title, it might be wise to consider the worst-case scenario.'

'Which is?'

'Theft of proprietary information, information that can be leveraged to extort large sums of money from your company or—'

'Be sold to one of our competitors,' Mr. Porter finished. He began pacing. 'Can we prove it?'

'It depends on your definition of proof.'

He stopped pacing and gave her a stern look. He could be formidable when he wanted to be. 'Confirmation, Ms. Sorensen. I'm asking for confirmation, plain and simple.'

'It is actually a little more complicated than that. There aren't many rules to this game, Mr. Porter, you can play it however you like but there are some things you should know going in.'

'Such as?'

'For one thing, every time I touch a computer, I change it. Every keystroke, every mouse click. If we go at this like a bull in a china closet, you'll get your confirmation one way or another, but you might also find yourself in a tight spot if you wind up in court.'

'How's that?'

'The admissibility of digital evidence can be tricky. And that's the nice way of saying it. Proving a crime is a lot simpler out here in the real world than it is in court so you have to decide now how you plan to use the information once you have it.'

Mr. Porter started pacing again and grumbled. 'That's a lot to ask when we don't even know what we're dealing with yet.'

'You just hit the nail on the head. Up till now, all I've done is look. Just enough to get a sense of what's there.' She gestured to the computer sitting under the desk. 'Now I have to start touching things. The risk of compromising evidence is greater. You're basically looking at the difference between straight-up incident response and the more calculated techniques of computer forensics. How we approach it depends on the kind of options you want available to you down the line.'

He raked his hand over what little hair he had on his head before coming to halt. 'What do you recommend?'

'Well, *normally*, I would expect to find some trace of malware activity flagged in the logs. I would expect to see alerts and packet captures being generated by the intrusion detection system. There's a goldmine of information in those resources. But if those things existed in this case, then surely your IT department would have jumped on this a long time ago.'

His faced darkened. 'Yes, well, you're probably used to working with a crew that knows what they're doing. Karen Forrester has feathered her nest with imbeciles and that's a fact.'

Dana cleared her throat and tried to tactfully steer around his ire.

'Since the application is already established,' she said, 'it would be a relatively simple thing to begin monitoring network traffic. Based on your earlier statements, your system has been affected by whatever this is for several weeks—it may be reasonable to let it continue for a short period of time in order to get a clearer picture of how the malware is actually behaving.'

Mr. Porter was skeptical. 'So you're recommendation is that I just let it go for now?'

She tread carefully. 'Most enterprise networks are affected by some type of malware almost all the time. I'm not saying it isn't a big deal because it *is* a big deal but, frankly, the more information we have, the better.'

Mr. Porter remained doubtful but he said nothing so she pressed on.

'We could learn a lot about the nature of the application in a short period of time,' she explained, 'simply by analyzing the communication between your computer and the remote system. We would also be able to determine if your system is being used as an entry point into the larger network.'

'And then?'

'We'll have a better understanding of the application's purpose. How the application is being leveraged, why it was introduced to your computer in the first place. And, if information is being siphoned out of your network, I might even be able to show you a snapshot of what's being taken.'

He nodded. 'Well, that would certainly come in handy for damage control but why not just figure out what it is first?'

'Network traffic is like a conversation—once it's gone, it's gone. The only way to preserve it is to capture it like a recording. The longer we wait, it's just that much more evidence lost. And, frankly, I'd rather not risk having someone on the remote end cut us off if they happen to catch on to what we're up to.'

'Can they do that?'

'It depends on how we go about it but, yes, they can.'

'How long will this take?'

'It's too early to tell but, conservatively, I'd say several days.'

Mr. Porter swore and reached around her to pick up the phone. He dialed a number and waited.

'Bob's not answering,' he groused before he hung up and turned to look at her. 'This is exactly the sort of thing that can turn into a PR disaster overnight.' He crossed his arms and leaned against the edge of his desk, thinking.

'So let me get this straight,' he said at last. 'You're telling me I can let the fire burn and maybe have enough evidence to involve the courts—hell, maybe even call in the cavalry—or I can put out the fire, toss the ashes, and hope for the best?'

'That's one way to put it.'

He shook his head. 'I get what you're driving at but, as far as I'm concerned, our woes are nobody's business. There's no way we're drawing attention to ourselves by taking this to court. And if someone is spying on me, I don't want it going any further. Can you figure out what this thing is, even if it's offline?'

Dana nodded. 'The basic functionality of it, sure. Although I could give you a more thorough analysis if you called in your IT staff.'

He laughed a short, bitter laugh. 'I don't want them anywhere near this. They could be the culprits for all I know.'

She couldn't argue with that. It certainly wouldn't be the first time an IT administrator was guilty of industrial espionage.

'I appreciate your concerns, Mr. Porter, but it's important you understand you *will* lose all the data stored in volatile memory as soon as I shut the power off. And it's worth thinking about because there's a lot of good stuff stored in RAM.' She paused to let that sink in. 'I have a tool that will let me capture that data but it requires someone with administrative privileges to run it.'

Mr. Porter smiled. It was the smile a grandfather bestowed on a favorite grandchild. 'If I didn't know better, Ms. Sorensen, I'd say you were trying to save me from myself.' He sobered. 'But here's the truth of it. If that woman gets involved, you're liable to walk away with nothing. She's just that wily. And I'd rather have half an answer than none at all.' He crossed his arms and nodded in the direction of his computer. 'Whatever this thing is, I want it stopped. Sooner rather than later.'

Dana didn't like the idea of leaving so many questions unanswered. If it was up to her, she'd want to know every gory detail before making her move, even if she had to plough Karen Forrester into the ground to do it. A defensive strategy made life easier today but it did nothing to protect an organization from being blindsided by the enemy tomorrow. She sighed. Time to buck up. The client was in charge and he'd made his choice—all she had to do was her job.

She studied the computer screen, weighing her options. A skillful attacker may never write files to the actual disk. On the outside chance that was the case here, she'd need the information stored in memory or her ship was already sunk. There had to be another way to get at it before she turned the power off.

She wracked her brain. There was always more than one way. How would she have done this before live acquisition was an option? She thought about what naturally occurring event might result in a memory dump. It was a short list. The Blue Screen of Death was *not* an option. If one bull in a china closet was bad, two was worse.

Hibernation, however, was an entirely different matter. It was similar to shutting the system down, except, in hibernation mode, the OS would restore everything just as it was when the power was turned off. To the user, it looked like nothing changed. Documents that were open would still be open, applications would still be up and running. But that was just an illusion. The OS wasn't holding everything in place, it was putting it all back, something that can only be achieved by writing back into memory what was there before. It may have been designed as a power management feature, a mere convenience, but, today, she was going to use it as a forensic tool.

Best of all, it was an easy task. All she had to do was choose 'hibernate' from the drop-down box and let the OS go to work. She sat back and waited for the shut down sequence to complete. Later, she would create a copy of the drive and convert the hidden file, hyberfil.sys, into something usable. If it worked as well as she hoped, she'd be able to analyze the contents of his physical memory as though she'd captured it live.

Once the CPU was finally untethered, she scrambled to her feet and squatted to lift it off the floor. It wasn't the heaviest she'd ever lugged around but it was bulky, almost more than the length of her arms could handle. She was slowly feeling her way around the desk when a sharp female voice boomed from somewhere on the far side of the room. Dana swore. It was Karen. She and Mr. Porter were busted.

'And just what is it that you think you're doing?' Karen demanded.

Dana angled her head around the case to see her standing in the doorway, hands on hips.

'I'm taking this computer downstairs for analysis,' she replied with the greatest amount of innocence she could rally. 'Possible malware.'

She left it at that. The cool metal edges of the case were pressing into her skin and she could feel her arms and lower back beginning to organize in protest. The less talking, the better.

Karen crossed her elegant arms and planted herself in the doorway. 'I don't doubt your expertise, Ms. Sorensen, but there's really no need for you to exert yourself like this. You should have called me. Had I known there was a problem, I would have gladly sent a technician up to do whatever needed to be done.'

Mr. Porter stepped into the fray. 'Now you just hold your horses. Those technicians you got down there aren't gonna do a damn thing to my computer and that's final. I'm the one who called Ms. Sorensen up here and if there's something that needs fixin', *she's* gonna be the one to fix it.'

Karen looked at Dana. 'Is that right? And just what is it that you're going to fix?'

Dana heaved her load up onto Mr. Porter's desk. 'Well, that depends. If it is what I think it is, then I'll be removing spyware.'

Karen arched an elegant eyebrow. 'Spyware? I highly doubt that. Mr. Porter is the president of this company. If there was something like that on his system, we would be aware of it.' She changed her stance to lean casually against the door frame. 'I don't know what you *think* you found but it's probably just one of our proprietary applications.'

'You may be right,' Dana conceded despite Mr. Porter's violent sputtering to the contrary. 'Assuming, of course, you have applications that run in the background, listening on unusual port numbers. You wouldn't happen to know of anything like that, would you?'

Karen didn't immediately respond but Dana could see the wheels turning. No doubt she was running through every possible move in her head, choosing the one with the most desired outcome. Question was, what outcome was a woman like Karen Forrester hoping for?

'Suppose there was something suspicious on his computer,' Karen said at last. 'How do you plan to prove it?'

Dana shrugged. 'Isolate the suspect file. Break it down. Analyze the functions. Run it through a disassembler, a debugger. I suppose decoding isn't out of the question, but, frankly, that doesn't seem likely. Unless, of course, you want to assign it to one of your own techs, in which case I can just leave it with you and go back to my desk.'

No longer leaning against the door frame, Karen ignored that last statement and made a show of inspecting her manicure.

'Fine. But I expect a full report in my inbox before you leave each night.' She stared at Dana. 'And don't even think about opening that case until I have a copy of a signed non-disclosure agreement on my desk.'

Having said her peace, Karen nodded a stiff goodbye to Mr. Porter and turned on her heel to glide past an angry-looking Grace. There was a full minute of silence before Mr. Porter spoke.

'I hate that woman,' he announced. 'She's nothing at all like her father. He and I went to school together, you know.' He looked to where Karen had been standing and shook his head. 'This is exactly what happens when you allow nepotism in the workplace.'

Dana staggered into Bennie's office clutching Mr. Porter's computer like a sleeping child, her bag slung across her back. She stumbled toward the desk, feeling for the edge as she went. When she was finally free of her burden, she flung her bag onto the floor and vigorously rubbed the deep grooves left in her skin by the the case. She thought about everything that just happened and groaned audibly. Floretta will be so pleased. Her first official day on the job and she was already knee-deep in horseshit.

She stripped off her jacket and kicked her shoes off onto the floor before easing into Bennie's chair. Almost immediately, her phone began buzzing angrily from somewhere in the recesses of her bag, something it had been doing off and on all afternoon. She wanted to ignore it but she hadn't bothered to return so much as a single text message all day and, in this hyper-connected age, that alone was enough to send most of the people she knew into a panic. Besides, if she dared miss another call from Floretta, she'd probably get stuck organizing this year's Christmas party.

It took some digging and she jammed her index finger into the side of her laptop but she got to the phone before it went to voicemail. Mazie's name popped up on the screen. She accepted the call as she flexed and straightened her sore finger.

'Hey Maze, how's it going?'

'Hey, you finally answered! I've been trying to call you for the last two hours. Is everything okay?'

Satisfied her finger was uninjured, Dana let her hand drop to her side.

'No, everything is *not* okay. In fact, I'm pretty sure I've been stranded on the wrong side of the river Styx.' She leaned back in the chair and rested her feet on the desk. 'How about you?'

Mazie could barely keep the excitement out of her voice. ' *Well*, I had lunch with my mom today and you'll never guess what we talked about!'

'You had lunch with your mother? On purpose?' Velma Reid was a force of nature unto herself, just like her daughter. They got along great so long as they weren't in the same room. 'How'd that go?'

'Lunch with mom? It went fine—well, mostly fine—but that's not the point. The point is that she knows Bennie's mother! It turns out she's known Sharon Price since, like, second grade or something. They hadn't seen each other in years but when mom saw Bennie's obituary in the paper, she made a casserole and paid Sharon a visit.'

Dana vaguely remembered Mazie saying Bennie grew up in that neck of the woods. All things considered, it made sense that Velma would have some connection. She knew every family that lived on a dirt road within fifty miles of her front porch in all directions. A terrible thought suddenly formed in Dana's mind.

'Oh God, Maze, you didn't tell her about Bob and Detective Mercer and the whole possible murder thing, did you?'

'Are you kidding? I am as smart as I look, you know. Besides, you know as well as I do the woman doesn't shut up long enough for anyone to get a word in edgewise. When would I have told her?'

'Good point,' replied Dana, letting out a sigh of relief. There was no telling what it would do to Bennie's mother if she found out a couple of amateurs were poking around in her son's business. 'So Velma knew about Bennie's death before we did?'

'She never said anything about it to me because she didn't think I'd be interested. He was quite a bit younger than us and she never knew he worked at BDS.'

'So what did she say about him?'

'Mostly stuff we already knew. Except for one thing. Did you know he had an anxiety disorder? According to mom, he took some pretty intense meds for it.'

Dana sat up straighter. Velma was a nurse so she would certainly know. 'I had no idea. So what does that have to do with his death? Don't people who commit suicide usually suffer from depression?'

'Ah, but that's the thing. He died from a lethal combination of his prescription medication and alcohol. And he had to have known about the risks because, according to Mrs. Price, he was always careful about it.'

Dana didn't like where this was heading. 'That doesn't necessarily mean it was intentional,' she ventured.

'You mean it could have been an accidental overdose?'

'Why not?'

'Well, I suppose anything is possible but don't accidental overdoses happen because people don't understand the risks of combining one substance with another? I think we already ruled that out in this case.'

'We don't know, he could've had a drug problem. Maybe he was abusing it and got carried away?'

'I doubt it. Mom asked about it—you know, the way she does—and Mrs. Price said she didn't think so, he had refills left. Some that were about to expire, too.'

'It doesn't make sense that he would allow that to happen if he was addicted to his meds,' Dana agreed. 'So what about the police investigation? Did she say anything about that?'

'It didn't come up but I'm sure Mrs. Price would have mentioned it.'

Dana sagged against the chair. Mazie was right. These were God-fearing country people. They would never call it suicide if they thought they could call it anything else.

'Thanks for letting me know, Maze. I've been hitting nothing but dead ends here and now I think I know why.'

'You think there's nothing to find?'

'Is there a better explanation?'

'I'm sorry, kiddo. I never thought I'd ever hear myself say this but I almost wish he *was* murdered. Under the circumstances, it seems nicer than the truth. Do you want to meet up for dinner later to talk about it?'

'No, I think I'll just go home tonight and soak in the tub. Maybe tomorrow?'

'Okie doke. See you then.'

Dana ended the call and let the phone drop into her lap. She barely had time to collect her thoughts before she was interrupted by a soft voice.

'Knock, knock. Is this a bad time?'

Dana looked up to see Ruby standing in the doorway and waved her in. 'No, no, it's not a bad time. I was just thinking, as usual.' She sat up straighter in the chair. 'So how did your research project go? Any luck?'

'I ran a query on everything that was either assigned to Bennie or submitted by him over the last 90 days,' replied Ruby, holding out a stack of printouts. 'I hope it's okay that I sorted everything chronologically.'

'Chronological is great,' said Dana, accepting the documents.

There was more there than she'd expected. Too bad it would probably turn out to be a waste of time.

She set the papers aside and looked at Ruby. She was a slight little thing, the very picture of femininity but without the curves. There was a general sadness, too. She cared more for Bennie than she let on, Dana was sure of it. She wasn't just grieving the loss of a friend, she was grieving the loss of what could've been. Dana was all too familiar with that particular burden.

'What do you know about malware analysis?' she blurted.

Ruby stammered, clearly caught off guard by the change in subject. 'Malware analysis? I don't guess I know anything about it. Why?'

Dana smiled and stood up to move Mr. Porter's computer to the center of the desk. It landed with a soft thud. 'Because, starting tomorrow, you're going to help me get to the bottom of what's ailing this system.'

Ruby blushed furiously. 'Are you sure? I mean, I don't know how much help I can be.'

'Do you like to solve puzzles?'

'Puzzles? You mean like Sudoku and cryptograms? Sure I do. Doesn't everybody?'

'No, actually, they don't. But if you like solving puzzles, then you'll *love* malware analysis.'

'What about Karen? Do you think she'll allow it?'

'I don't know. I wasn't planning to ask.'

The elevator doors opened on the ground floor and Bob

wheeled out into the stark, gray hallway that led to the IT department. He rarely came down here but Dana had left him no choice. She wasn't replying to his text messages and now there was this business with Sam. The woman owed him an explanation.

He maneuvered through the double doors that stood at the entrance of Karen's domain and slipped past the mostly empty cubicles without being noticed. Karen's light was already out. He checked his watch. She'd left early, which was unusual for her.

He hesitated just outside Bennie's office, struck by the image of Dana sitting there in his stead. She looked exactly the same. As plain as plain could be, she revealed her beauty only through her expressiveness and intelligence. And no one could resist her when she did. Especially him.

'Are you just gonna sit there and stare or did you have something you wanted to say?' she asked, never taking her eyes off the screen in front of her.

He eased into the room and deftly spun around to shut the door behind him before engaging the lock. He didn't want any interruptions. When he turned back to face her, he was met with a pair of brown eyes gazing at him speculatively.

'I'm not going to have sex with you if that's what you're thinking,' she quipped.

'That's not why I'm here, but maybe we can try that next time,' he countered, eying the top of the desk suggestively.

She blushed and looked away. The satisfaction he felt at her reaction was overwhelming but now was not the time to indulge in fantasies.

'I actually came to talk about Sam,' he said.

She shrugged, still unwilling to look at him. 'There's not much to tell. It's too early to know anything for sure.'

'But you think there's a legitimate cause for concern.'

'Yes,' she replied unapologetically.

He nodded his head, waiting for her to launch into the details. She didn't. He decided to switch gears. 'So what have you learned so far about Bennie?'

'I could ask you the same thing.' She finally made eye contact with him. 'Did you know he was taking medication to manage an anxiety disorder? Medication he knew could be fatal when combined with alcohol?'

'Where did you hear that?' he demanded.

Her eyes flashed. 'So you *did* know.'

He swore. 'Yes, I knew. So what?'

Dana snapped her laptop lid closed and reached for her bag. 'I get it, Bob. I really do. No one wants to think it's possible that someone they care about could do something so selfish but sometimes they just do.' She stood up. 'Even you have to admit suicide is the simplest explanation in this case, no matter how questionable the circumstances.'

He watched as she prepared to make a run for it but he wasn't about to let her escape. Not this time.

'Selfish is a strong word. Is that what you think of Bennie or is that what you think of me?'

'What's that supposed to mean?' she snapped.

'You know exactly what I mean.' He swore softly. 'Look, I

know you don't believe it but I never meant to hurt you. Christ, at the time, I thought I was doing it *for* you. For both of us.' He took a breath. 'But that wasn't Bennie's way.'

'I would've said that about you once upon a time but it didn't stop you from trying.'

He stifled a groan. The pounding in his head was back, his own private scourge ever since the accident. He could still hear the scream of the breaks to this day, the glass as it shattered. He could see the brightness of the operating room when he closed his eyes. And the endless darkness that followed.

'It was different for me,' he said, locking eyes with her. 'I had something to run from. Bennie didn't. Please don't give up, not yet.'

She flinched but held her composure. That was his Dana, always in control. He could see the question in her eyes, the pain of it. *Was he running from her?* But she didn't ask. He wondered if he would have the guts to tell her the truth if she did.

'I can't make any promises,' she said instead, looking at her hands.

'I'm not asking you to.'

She hauled in a breath. 'Fine. But I need more time.' She gestured to the piles of papers stacked around the room. 'Bennie didn't exactly leave a trail of breadcrumbs.'

He nodded but swore inwardly. He looked around. The office looked like it had been professionally tossed. Dana didn't miss anything. But she hadn't seen everything. He thought about the notes locked away in his office. He and Bennie had played a dangerous game. A game they'd been winning, until now. He closed his eyes. He needed answers. Question was, how much would he have to reveal to get them?

'You're bound to run across something sooner or later,' he said, more to himself than to her. 'Maybe you can use this thing with Sam to your advantage.'

She snorted. 'I don't see how. Not unless you think his problem is somehow related.'

'Don't kid yourself. Sam likes you. And despite what you've seen, that means something. If Karen's still standing, it's because he hasn't decided to knock her down.'

His phone vibrated. It was Sam.

'Speaking of the devil.' He slipped his phone back into his pocket. 'I better get up there. By the way, did you actually read any of my text messages?'

She rolled her eyes. 'What *is* this global fascination with texting? *Yes*, I read the messages. I just haven't had time to reply yet.'

He suppressed a smile. She was lying. 'So we're good to go?'

'Sure, fine, whatever. *We're good to go.* Now will you leave me alone so I can work? I have all this crap to do before I can leave and I still need to swing by my office tonight.'

He didn't need to be told twice. If he hung around, she might actually check her phone and realize her error. He unlocked the door and wheeled back the same way he came, careful to avoid being seen. He punched the elevator call button on the wall and smiled to himself, the pain in his head all but forgotten. He may not have gotten what he came for but, somehow, he got exactly what he wanted.

Dana watched the door close behind Bob on his way out. He seemed happy. Too happy, considering what just went down. What was he up to? She reached into her bag for her phone and scrolled through her text messages until she found the conversation she was looking for.

> 9:42AM, Aug 18: need to set up meeting, pls call me asap
> 11:58AM, Aug 18: where r u?
> 2:04PM, Aug 18: no call, no input
> 3:37PM, Aug 18: fine, meet @ my place, 7pm tomorrow

His place? No wonder the little turd was smiling. He totally baited her and she walked right into it. There was no way she was letting him get the upper hand so easily. She typed in a reply and hit send:

> 4:53PM, Aug 18: it's a date, c u there

He said he had something to run from, let him run from that. Now all she had to do was figure out where he lived.

She hoisted the strap of her bag up onto her shoulder and checked the time on her phone. If she left for BDS now, she might make it home before midnight. She didn't get far before she heard the sound of paper scattering to the floor. She groaned. She'd entirely forgotten about the printouts Ruby had given her.

She turned around and began plucking the pages off the gray carpeting, one at a time. So much for all Ruby's hard work putting them into chronological order. One of the pages had slipped into the shadows under the desk. She eased her shoulders into the dark space to reach for it and felt something graze the top of her head. There wasn't enough light to see much but she could feel a slight bulge. Whatever it was, it was firmly fixed to the underside of the desk.

She pulled a pair of scissors from the center drawer and carefully pried the object loose. It turned out to be a composition-style notebook similar to the ones she used in grade school. It wasn't that unusual to find things stuck to the bottom of a desk— it was always one of the first places she looked for passwords—but an entire notebook was a first.

She cut away the rest of the tape and flipped through several pages of neatly blocked notes interspersed with handwritten tables. Sketches of various objects and characters—mostly superheroes and their weapons of choice—were scattered in the margins. It was the diary of a 12-year-old boy, only it wasn't. The passages were jumbled. She recognized an old-fashioned substitution cipher when she saw one but it looked complicated. What had Bennie gotten himself into that made him feel like he needed to encrypt his notes and then conceal them?

She swore softly. Her intuition knew what her brain did not. Bennie had gotten himself into a pile of trouble and, somehow, she needed to find out why.

CHAPTER FOUR

Something Big

Dana pressed her employee ID badge up against the glass at the front entrance of Bellwether Data Security and waited for one of the security guards to let her in. Lights were still on in the building but, by this hour, more people were leaving out the side doors than coming in through the front. She wished she could be one of them.

Stan, a regular night guard, met her at the door and she handed him a cup carrier loaded with cold drinks from Sonic and a bag of burgers that had been precariously wedged under her arm.

The older man feigned surprise. 'What's this? A gift from our favorite analyst?'

She grinned.

'So who are you trying to avoid this time?' he asked, taking the food and drinks under one arm and pulling the door shut behind her with the other.

'Everyone. I need to get some work done.'

He smiled. 'No problem. But you know we can't help you if a, uh, *certain someone* checks the logs.'

She knew he meant Floretta. 'I'll just have to risk it,' she replied, slipping her badge back into the plastic sleeve clipped to her shirt. 'So who's working the labs tonight?'

'Alex called in so Eli's covering for him. I'll let him know you're on your way up.'

She thanked him and waved hello to the other guards manning the desk before punching the elevator button to head up to the third floor where the labs were located. The elevator opened to an enclosure with a set of double doors on one end that led to a network of rooms used for short-term storage and processing of evidence. The entire floor was a restricted access area so the doors could only be opened from inside by authorized lab personnel.

There were cameras positioned at multiple angles to provide a clear view of the entire enclosure with a close-up camera mounted near the door. She waved to Eli through the camera and promptly heard a buzz, which signaled that the door lock was disengaged for her entry. He met her just a few feet in and she was reminded what a beautiful specimen of a man he really was. Eli Goodfox was only half Native American but he looked every inch like the real deal. The real deal with a lithe, strong body and a full head of shining black hair that fell effortlessly just past his shoulders. It was no wonder that Mazie was half in love with him.

She mentally shook herself and plastered what she hoped was a friendly-but-not-too-friendly smile on her face. 'Is there a lab available? I need to image a drive.'

Eli returned her smile in a way that made her wonder if he

could tell what she'd been thinking. No doubt he was accustomed to women swooning in his presence.

'Sure thing,' he said. 'But you'll have to use a write blocker. The Image MASSters are tied up right now.'

'All of them? Are you sure?'

'Afraid so,' he replied, leading her to an office just off the main hallway. 'Things just happen to be really hectic right now.'

He sat down in front of a wall of computer screens showing various locations in and around the lab. There were more people on the floor than she thought there'd be.

'How many people are here tonight?' she asked.

'Including you? Five. Nothing major going on, though. Drew is working a high-priority porn case but that's about as interesting as it gets.' He flipped open his log book. 'So it looks like all I have left is room 307B. Do you have a case number for me?'

Dana pulled the client file out of her bag and handed it to him. He flipped it open, scanned for what he was looking for, and handed it back before rifling through a pile of proximity cards in a drawer.

'Are you planning to transfer custody of anything before you leave?' he asked, giving her one of the cards.

She shook her head. 'Not this time. I'm storing everything at the client site for now.'

'Sounds like you're all set then. I'll be in here, holding down the fort, if you need anything. By the way,' he added, 'how's Mazie doing? I can't remember the last time I saw her come through here.'

She couldn't resist a grin. Mazie was going to go nuts when she heard about this. 'She's doing great. Up to no good, as usual. I'll tell her you said hi.'

Eli smiled. She thought she detected something in his eyes— was it shyness?—but it was gone in an instant. Still, though, an idea formed in her mind. She just hoped Mazie would cooperate.

She headed down the hall and took the first left. It was a circuitous path to 307B. As soon as she rounded the last corner, she heard assorted grunts and moans and the not-so-subtle sounds of skin slapping on skin. That would be Drew and his high-priority porn case. Poor guy. Most people mistakenly assumed that spending hours on end looking at porn was one of the perks of the job but, in reality, it was the exact opposite. There were a lot of strange and disturbing things in the world and, eventually, they all ended up in a place like this being looked at by people like her. And none of it, once seen, could ever be unseen.

307B was as far from where she started as she could possibly get. She waved the prox card in front of the reader mounted on the wall near the door handle and the door popped open. The room itself wasn't much bigger than a supply closet but it was tidy and, from the looks of things, had what she needed.

Just before she left GES, she'd pulled Mr. Porter's hard drive and slipped it into an anti-static evidence bag. Now, she carefully removed it and set it on the workbench. She revved up the forensic workstation and dug around in the various bins and drawers until she found the stash of hardware write blockers. Conveniently, the one she needed was right on top.

The write blocker would prevent the forensic workstation from writing any data to the drive during the imaging process. Without it, even a simple action like connecting it to a computer would result in some small change that could prove disastrous in court. And despite Mr. Porter's insistence that GES would not take legal action, she knew from experience how quickly that could change.

She sifted through another drawer for a blank external hard drive sufficiently large enough to hold a bit for bit, raw image of Mr. Porter's drive and connected it to the workstation. Using imaging software to copy the contents of one drive to the other would take about three hours to complete but her reward would be an exact copy of Mr. Porter's hard drive that she could explore freely, preserving the original for some other, as yet unknown, purpose.

In a matter of minutes, the software was hard at work. There was nothing for her to do but wait. She leaned back in the chair and let the mechanical sounds of the hard drive platters fill her head. The whirring and spinning was soothing in its own way. It was methodical, like a softly ticking clock. She rubbed her eyes and tried to ignore the fatigue that washed over her. Anymore, it seemed like every day was a long day.

Looking for a way to keep herself occupied, she pulled out Bennie's notebook. She splayed it out on the table and flipped through the pages, more slowly this time, studying them, looking for patterns. She was struck by how little she had known about him as a person. She never would've pegged him as a student of classical cryptography, that's for sure. His technique was arguably old-fashioned but he was smart about it. No spaces between words, every line had the same number of characters, no obvious repeats.

He'd used every letter of the English alphabet so, clearly, he wasn't using a code. And yet it was too complicated to be a simple substitution cipher—it would be obvious if he was using just one set of characters. Her best guess, then, was that he'd devised some kind of Vigenère square, a polyalphabetic substitution cipher once thought to be unbreakable.

But it was breakable. A computer could do the work in a matter of minutes—and, fortunately, there was no shortage of those around here.

Dana was dozing comfortably, her feet propped up on the workbench, when a sound jolted her awake. Bennie's notebook had fallen from her lap onto the floor. She checked the time on her phone, wondering how long she'd been asleep. It was just after 10:30, not as late as she thought.

The hard drives connected to the forensic workstation were silent. The imaging process had stopped. Yawning loudly, she wiggled the mouse to get rid of the screen saver and examined her progress. The process was complete; moreover, she had a set of hash values.

The hash value was calculated by feeding the entire contents of the hard drive into an algorithm that generated a unique number value, creating a sort of digital fingerprint. Changing even one bit of the original data would result in a completely different hash value, making it a useful comparison tool. Auspiciously, the hash values of Mr. Porter's hard drive and the image she'd just created were identical. Down to the smallest detail, one was an exact copy of the other. She could finally go home.

She rifled through her things for another anti-static evidence bag to hold the external device that now held the copy of Mr. Porter's hard drive. She bundled it with a chain of custody form and carefully packed it along with the original evidence drive. Both drives were going home with her for the night—tomorrow, they'd find a permanent home at GES.

She swung the door open to go check out with Eli and came face to face with Floretta, who was just as startled to see Dana as Dana was to see her. The two women danced around precariously until Dana finally managed to find safe footing back inside the confines of 307B.

'What are you doing here?' she demanded, genuinely surprised to see Floretta skulking around at this time of night.

'I could ask you the same thing,' Floretta retorted. 'I've been sending you messages all damn day, asking you to come by my office. I haven't seen hide nor hair of you, only to come down here to check on Drew and find out you're right under my damn nose.'

Dana swore. Floretta had her cornered and she knew it.

Floretta was relentless. 'Oh, yes, baby girl, this is happening so you may as well get comfortable.' She swept past Dana and helped herself to the lone chair in the room. 'So, tell me, how did it go today at GES?'

Dana arched an eyebrow, already suspicious of where the conversation was headed. Floretta knew perfectly well how things were going at GES. Knowing things was her superpower.

'It went fine,' she lied. 'Better than expected.'

Floretta narrowed her eyes. 'Is that why you're availing yourself of the labs at this hour and doing your damnedest to hide from me?'

'I'm not hiding, I'm working.'

'Bullshit. You're hiding.'

Dana said nothing so Floretta continued. 'Let me make this easy for you. I know Bob has you on a wild goose chase, trying to get to the bottom of what happened to that poor boy, and I know the OKCPD came knocking on your door this morning. I also know that you pissed off the IT director at your new gig somethin' fierce and landed yourself in the middle of a feud between her and that little round man who's in charge over there.' She stopped to assess Dana's reaction. 'Have I missed anything so far?'

Dana was dumbfounded. 'How many spies do you have in this world?'

'Apparently not enough to keep you out of trouble, which is why I've decided to have you and Max swap places. He'll take over at GES starting tomorrow and you can pick up with whatever the hell it is that he's working on.'

Dana was livid. 'Are you shitting me? You forced me into this and now you want to pull me out and give it over to Max? Absolutely not. This is my case and I finish what I start. You can just tell Max to slither back into whatever hole he came from.'

Floretta looked at Dana for a full minute, her face impossible to read. 'You're sure about this?' she said at last.

Dana didn't blink. 'Yes.'

'What about Bob?'

'What about him? He's on board with what I'm doing, if that's what you're asking.'

'That's not what I'm asking.'

Dana looked away. 'It's a little awkward,' she admitted. 'We'll make do.'

'You must be in one helluva mess if you're willing to get the old team back together again.'

'We're not back together,' Dana protested.

'I feel like I've heard that before.'

'He tried to commit suicide, Floretta. That's not something a girl forgets.'

'Or forgives,' observed Floretta, unapologetically. 'Why is that, do you suppose? I mean, is it really any wonder that he might try to end his own life after everything that happened to him? A big, strappin' man like that suddenly dealing with life in a wheelchair—all those surgeries—all because some idiot teenager couldn't keep his hands off his damn cell phone. I can't imagine what he must've been going through, how he must've suffered.'

'He wasn't going through it alone,' insisted Dana. 'He was surrounded by people who loved him.'

'And thank goodness for that, too. I hate to think what might've happened if you hadn't found him in time.'

'I wasn't supposed to find him in time, Flo. I came home early.'

Floretta snorted. 'We've discussed this. He knew you were coming home early and, whether you choose to believe it or not, that means something.'

'He was leaving me,' blurted Dana. 'He was just using pills to do it. He was leaving me and he didn't even bother to write a note explaining why. Are you happy now?'

Floretta blinked. 'So that's what's got you so upset? That he was leaving you without saying goodbye? So why is it, then, that the only person who actually went anywhere was you?'

Dana said nothing. The last thing she needed was Floretta in her head and she'd said too much as it was. But Floretta wasn't finished.

'You know what I think? I think this isn't about Bob at all. This is about someone else who left you without saying goodbye, isn't it. And now, all these years later, you're making Bob pay for it.'

'You don't know what you're talking about,' whispered Dana, unwilling to look Floretta in the eye.

Floretta stood and pulled an envelope out of her jacket pocket. 'You're a stubborn son of a gun, you know that? I'm not your mother and I don't have the right to tell you how to live your life, but you learn a few things by the time you get to be my age so I'm gonna tell it to you anyway. No one is keeping score, baby girl. No one. The only thing any of us can ever leave the world with is what we carry around inside us. Climb the career ladder all you want, make as much money as you want, hell, you can even become famous if you want—none of it will ever amount to a hill of beans. The real value is in our experiences, in our relationships, in how much we allow ourselves to care. And no matter how hard you fight it, forgiveness is a part of that.' She handed Dana the envelope. 'You live the life you choose, baby girl, so choose wisely.'

Dana looked at the unmarked envelope in her hand, confused. 'What's this?'

'Open it and find out,' said Floretta as she breezed out the door. 'And think about what I said.'

Alone again, curiosity getting the best of her, Dana tore open the envelope and was immediately stunned by its contents. It contained a single-page document, printed front and back.

Dear Ms. Sorensen... We are pleased to offer you the position of Vice President of Consumer Services... based on your exemplary job performance and superior peer reviews... if the terms of this offer are acceptable to you, please sign the reverse page of this letter and return it to Human Resources no later than September 1st... signed Jeremy Stiles, Senior Vice President, Consumer Services.

How could this be? There was no interview. She'd barely even spoken to Jeremy Stiles in all the years she'd been working at the company. If it was a popularity contest, Max should have been a shoo-in.

She closed her eyes and swore. *Floretta.* It had to be. There was no one else at Bellwether Data Security with her kind of influence.

Her heart pounded in her chest. She'd wanted this so badly. She'd *needed* this so badly. And here it was in black and white, her chance to get out of corporate services. No more field work, no more corporate bullshit, no more late nights in the lab, no more Max Chen, no more Floretta.

No more Floretta. It was a strange thought. If she was completely honest with herself, she wasn't sure if that was a good thing or a bad thing.

Dana plopped down in Bennie's chair the next morning, exhausted. The unsigned offer letter was burning a hole in her bag but she couldn't bring herself to do anything with it. It was all too fresh in her mind. She just needed a little time to let things settle. She'd finish this job, get some distance between her and Bob, and the rest would sort itself out naturally.

In the meantime, Mr. Porter needed some answers.

She was in the process of getting her laptop ready to go when Ruby bounded in with two coffees. The logo on the cups was from the stand downstairs.

'I hope you like caramel lattes,' she said, holding one out for Dana.

Dana accepted it with enthusiasm. A jolt of caffeine with a dose of sugar was just what she needed. 'I've never met a cup of coffee in my life I didn't like,' she said, taking a sip. It was delicious. 'You have no idea how much I needed this.'

Ruby blushed, caught off guard by Dana's sincerity. 'You're welcome,' she stammered. 'Are we still on for today?'

Dana was momentarily confused but then remembered her promise to let Ruby help. 'Yes! Are you ready to get started?

Ruby nodded eagerly and pulled the straight-backed chair closer to the desk to give herself a place to sit. Dana slid the external hard drive containing the forensic image out of her bag and placed it next to her laptop, along with a notepad and ink pen.

'This is a copy of the user's hard drive,' she explained. 'We always work with a copy to avoid damaging the original.'

She set her coffee cup way out of the way and angled the screen so Ruby could see what she was doing.

'We need to get the image mounted so we can actually work with it, and then we can take a look at the only lead we have so far, which happens to be the name of an executable file.'

Before she could mount anything, however, she needed to set up a virtual machine. Malware was unpredictable by nature. Until its function was understood, she had to assume it was capable of anything. Attempting to analyze it outside of a controlled environment could, therefore, prove disastrous.

A virtual machine, essentially a computer within a computer, had the benefit of being isolated from the actual operating system and underlying hardware of the computer it was running on, which meant that anything the malware did would have no effect outside the virtual environment. It wasn't foolproof, of course, because malware could be designed to detect a virtual environment—rendering virtual analysis difficult, if not impossible—but that was generally the exception and not the rule.

Since she used virtual machines in her work on a regular basis, she already had a number of presets on her laptop to choose from, which made mounting the image of Mr. Porter's drive a quick and easy process. Once properly mounted, the virtual machine would recognize the image as a physical drive like any other, and then it would just be a matter of locating the file of interest and beginning her analysis.

She turned back to Ruby, who, for her part, had been sitting patiently, watching.

'The first thing we need to do is isolate our file and begin with a basic static analysis, which just means that we'll look at the properties of the file without running it—and then we'll move on to a more dynamic analysis so we can see what it actually does.'

'How did you figure out what file to isolate?' asked Ruby.

It was a good question. Dana was impressed. The only other person she'd ever trained was Max and he always acted like he knew the answer to everything already. But that was Max, all about appearances. Ruby was different.

'In most cases,' she explained, 'there is some indication of where we should begin our search. It's fairly unusual to go into something like this with no information. A lot of times it comes from things like antivirus software or an intrusion detection system that flags unusual network behavior but, in this case, we're looking for something that was identified during a manual search.'

'So you could tell it was a bad file just by looking at it?'

'Not at all. Sometimes you just have to go with your gut. I guess you could say I made an educated guess.'

Ruby's eyebrows flew up. 'So it could turn out to be nothing?'

'Yup,' said Dana, grinning. 'See? I *told* you it would be fun.'

The easiest thing to do with potential malware was to simply bump it against as many antivirus programs as possible to see what turned up but she decided to forgo it on this occasion because the results were likely to be spotty and, at best, provide only generic information. GES equipped their systems with reasonably robust antivirus software—if it was as simple as that it wouldn't have gotten this far.

Like most Windows executables, CRE_pt10.exe contained a header with information about the code stored inside. Normally, this information would be used by the operating system but it was equally useful for someone with a software tool capable of parsing it.

The file header would tell her what kind of program it was, give her hints as to its functionality, and provide other invaluable clues that could help her better understand some of what she might see later in the process. In this case, the header indicated that the executable was compiled recently, in April.

The compile time wasn't necessarily the most reliable piece of information in a file header but it did seem to correlate with the timeline. She'd take it with a grain of salt, but it was likely that this particular executable was created four months ago.

'Make a note, will you Ruby? Find out when Mr. Porter started complaining about his system.'

'Which time? He's complained about his computer for as long as I've been here.'

Dana looked up. 'How long is that?'

'Almost five years.'

Dana shook her head. She should've known the man would be a paranoid compuchondriac.

'Just look for anything where he's specifically mentioned a

problem with his mouse and follow it back until you find the initial report,' she said.

Ruby scribbled a note on her little notepad as Dana clicked around some more in the file header.

'Well, I think we just solved another mystery,' she announced some seconds later. 'According to the this, it's a console program. That could explain the black boxes he described flashing up on his screen.'

Ruby's brows furrowed. 'The program runs in a command window?'

Dana nodded and pointed to the subsystem description on the screen. 'I'm also seeing where this program invokes a number of functions but nothing that explains the other behavior he mentioned.'

'Does that mean we're looking at the wrong file?' asked Ruby.

'It's more like we're looking at just one piece of the puzzle. And *that* means we need to be on the lookout for other files that go with this one.'

She decided to dig around in the resource section of the header, which typically contained various objects used by the executable that weren't actually part of the code, like image files and other design elements. This area was sort of like a junk drawer in that a programmer could use it to store pretty much anything they wanted, including other executable code. And by the looks of things, that was certainly the case here.

She looked up at Ruby and pointed to the screen again. 'It looks like this little executable's *real* job is to extract the code that's hidden inside the header.'

'A program inside of a program? Can it do that?'

'Neat little trick, isn't it.'

'So what do we do now?'

'Now we extract the embedded code so we can analyze it independently. If we really want to know what this thing does, that's where the answers will be.'

Bob checked his watch. Going on 10 AM and still no word from Dana. She may have wanted the final word last night but, today, in the bright sunlight, she was bound to rethink it. He fully expected her to cancel on him. He couldn't really blame her but, still, there was a part of him that wished she'd surprise him, just this once.

He looked out his office window, past the parking lot, to the brittle fields beyond. If not for the black-eyed Susans rising from the roadside ditches, with their bright yellow flowers clinging proudly to whatever shade there was, the landscape here would be completely shapeless. As far as he could tell, the only thing holding it all together was sheer stubbornness.

'It's a sad sight, ain't it?'

Startled, Bob turned sharply to see Sam standing in front of his desk.

Sam held up his hands in mock surrender. 'Didn't mean to sneak up on you. It just so happens Helen wasn't out front so I thought I'd let myself in.'

'Of course,' said Bob, wheeling around to sit behind his desk.

'You're welcome to come in whenever you want. I was just lost in thought is all.' He gestured to a chair. 'Please, have a seat. I don't know what I can offer you but I'm sure I can scrounge up a bottle of water or something.'

Sam hoisted himself into a chair and waved the idea away. 'No need for any of that. I just stopped in for a quick visit.'

'Something on your mind?'

'You could say that. Been talking to Dean.'

Bob stifled a groan. Dean Forrester was a pot-stirrer who always had his fingers in somebody else's pie, just like his daughter. There was no telling what fool's errand he'd sent Sam on this time. Bob braced himself.

'As you can imagine,' began Sam, 'he's very keen that Bennie Price's death not be connected with this company in any way.'

Bob leaned forward, suddenly confused. 'What are you talking about?'

'I'm *talking* about the real reason Ms. Sorensen is here,' replied Sam, somewhat impatiently.

Bob gripped the wheels of his chair, hard, but managed to maintain his composure. His senses warned him to be careful. To underestimate Sam Porter could be a dangerous thing.

'Listen,' he said, adopting as conciliatory a tone as he could manage, 'if Dean's worried that Dana will push his precious daughter out of a job, then you can tell him to forget about it. Dana wouldn't work for me if you offered her a million dollars a year.'

Sam wasn't amused. 'You think you can piss on my leg and tell me it's rainin'? Keep it up and see what happens.' He shifted in his chair. 'Now I don't know all the particulars and I don't care to, but this business of looking into Bennie's death has got to stop.'

'Why?' Bob challenged. 'Aren't you just as concerned as I am?'

'I most certainly am not,' sputtered Sam, his gaze not quite making contact with Bob's. 'And neither should you be. We have bigger fish to fry. This thing with Bennie is a waste of your time and it's not doing anybody a damn bit of good, yourself included.'

'Bennie was one of us,' replied Bob simply.

Sam's eyes flashed. 'Bennie was a traitor to this company,' he spat. 'Now he may not have deserved what he got but he brought it on himself.'

Bob was incredulous. 'How can you—'

Sam held up a hand to stop him. 'No, like it or not, this conversation is over. I love you like a son and that's the God's honest truth, but I cannot protect you from this. End this nonsense now.'

'So that's it? We're just supposed to forget it and move on?'

Sam stood to leave, finally looking Bob dead in the eye. 'Focus on the job at hand. No more, no less. And, for God's sakes, keep Ms. Sorensen on a short leash.'

Bob watched as Sam vanished through the doorway. Alone, consumed with rage, he slammed his fists into the solid oak desk. It boomed, he felt the joints begin to separate under the strain. He was always a strong man, stronger now from years of pushing himself around in a wheelchair. But strength wasn't going to win this fight.

He turned to look back over the fields that stretched into the horizon and the little yellow flowers that dotted the roadways. It wasn't strength he needed, it was stubbornness. And no matter what Dean Forrester might think, that was the real reason Dana was there.

Dana stretched and reached for her now-cold latte as she studied the long line of assembly language code on the screen in front of her. Ruby was still with her, though barely.

```
00007678      ...
00007679      push eax
0000767A      lea eax, [ebp+hKey]
0000767B      call ds:RegSetValueExW
0000767C      push 1
0000767D      push 0
0000767E      mov [ebp+var_4], eax
0000767F      ...
```

'How can you stand to look at it?' Ruby grumbled, her enthusiasm for the project clearly waning.

Dana smiled and gave a little shrug. 'Well, it'd be a whole lot worse if we were sitting here trying to make sense out of machine code.'

Ruby was unconvinced. And, although she'd never admit it, so was Dana. Assembly language was brutal. It was the best she could do under the circumstances, however.

Executable files were compiled from easy-to-read source code but were themselves comprised of binary, the machine code that was delivered directly into the processor. It was possible to reverse-engineer the program into human-readable form using a disassembler, but assembly language was as high as she could go reliably. To call it 'human-readable' might be a stretch but, for the initiated, it was decipherable.

'Don't give up on me now, kiddo, this is the puzzle I promised you,' she said, gesturing toward the screen. 'And these are the clues.'

Ruby strained to understand the short lines of instructions and screwed up her face. 'There are just so many! What am I looking for?'

'You're looking for common constructs. Small clusters of code that describe what the program is doing.'

'Do you see anything?'

Dana scrolled through several lines of code. In fact, she did see something.

'Do you see this section here?' she asked, pointing to the screen. 'This shows us where the program modifies the system's registry so that it will automatically run on startup, or at least it tries to. I'll have to look at the registry settings to see if it actually took.'

Ruby leaned in, her interest piqued.

'It's okay that you don't fully understand it,' Dana assured her. 'This is the kind of thing that takes a little study and a lot of practice.'

Dana turned her attention back to the screen and continued scrolling through the instructions, looking for areas of interest. As expected, CRE_pt10.exe loaded the code embedded in the resource header into memory and then executed it. No real surprise there.

Of greater interest was the presence of a function that created a new process that effectively redirected the embedded executable's input and output to a network socket.

She exited the disassembler software and launched a debugger. It was time to see this thing in action. It didn't take long to step through it as the program really only did three things—it set itself up to run every time the system was turned on, it executed the embedded code, and it established a remote shell. Straightforward, but troubling all the same.

She turned to Ruby. 'Are GES systems configured for remote access?'

Ruby blinked. 'Yes, but they can only accept remote connections from systems inside the network. We can't remote in from outside.'

Dana nodded slowly, letting the information float and then sink in. More troubling news.

She gave herself a mental shake. Having exhausted the usefulness of the first executable, she turned her attention to the second excutable that she generically named *embeddedCode*.

Several minutes later, she sat back in the chair with a frown.

'What is it?' Ruby asked.

Dana took a deep breath, unsure of how much she should reveal. 'We found something,' she said at last. 'Something big.'

CHAPTER FIVE

Easy as .py

Bob raked his hand through his hair and swore violently. 'Are you certain?'

Dana raised an eyebrow.

He closed his eyes and forced himself to focus. Of course she was certain. She wouldn't have come to his office otherwise.

'Your response is understandable but there's no mistake,' she said plainly. 'Somehow, someone managed to install a backdoor on Sam Porter's computer, along with a keylogger that's been dumping his keystrokes into a text file.'

A knot formed in the pit of his stomach. As president of the company, Sam was privy to everything. And he had Grace. If the man typed anything with his own two hands, it was guaranteed to be highly sensitive.

'How long has this been going on?'

Dana shook her head. 'Hard to say at this point. The program creates a new text file every time it runs. The old files are sent off to a remote system and then deleted from the local drive almost immediately. You could go by the compile time in April but—'

'That could just be whatever random date the attacker wanted it to be,' he finished. 'What about unallocated space? You can recover the deleted files from there and work backwards, right?'

She shrugged. 'I don't see why not. It's a massive hard drive, mostly unused. I'd be shocked to find much of anything that's been overwritten. But you realize, of course, that's only half the equation.'

Bob messaged his temples. He knew what she meant. The real question was whether the information had actually made its way to the remote system.

'What do we know about the remote host?' he asked.

'Next to nothing. I fished an IP address out of the code but nothing came back when I pinged it.'

He did a double-take. 'You sent an ICMP request? That's a little obvious, don't you think?

Her eyebrow shot up again. 'Stealth ceased to be an option as soon as your boss ordered me to unplug the box, *don't you think?*

He couldn't resist a smile. Man, he'd missed this. No matter how fast or how slow, she was never out of step.

'Besides,' she continued, 'I recognized it as a local IP address and thought, what the hell?'

His head snapped up. 'A local IP address. You mean it's one of ours?'

'Same network address but there's no documentation on it that I could find. I've asked Ruby to query the DHCP server to see if there's a record of it there.'

'Ruby's working with you on this?' His tone was sharper than he intended but it was suddenly all too clear they didn't know who they could trust. 'How much does she know?'

'She doesn't know what it is, if that's what you're asking. She spent part of the morning with me, observing, and then I sent her off to research the IP address.' Dana looked puzzled. 'Why? Is there something I should know?'

'No.' He sagged in his chair. 'Hell, I don't know. I don't know what I know anymore.'

'I don't understand. Is something wrong?'

Bob looked at her face. Her beautiful, expressive face, now etched with concern.

'Dean Forrester sent Sam in here this morning to warn me off. He doesn't want me looking into Bennie's death.'

'What does Sam say about it?'

'He says he can't protect me.'

Her concern deepened. 'Do you need protecting?'

'Well, now, that is the question, isn't it?' he replied, smiling ruefully.

She shifted uncomfortably, her head tilted slightly down. He studied her. If he didn't know better, he'd say she was withholding on him. 'Unless maybe you've finally found something of interest?' he prodded.

She looked up at him, her face suddenly unreadable. 'No,' she replied. 'But I'm working on it.'

He didn't push her any further. He couldn't. He'd asked more of her than he had a right to as it was.

He cleared his throat. 'So about tonight—'

'I've been meaning to ask you about that,' she interjected, reaching into her bag to pull out her phone. 'What's your address?'

'My address?'

She blinked. 'Yes, of course, your address. How will I find your house if I don't know where you live?'

He grinned. So the imp wasn't going to back out after all. He gave her the address and watched her face as she worked it out.

'You still live in our house?' she asked.

He shrugged. 'I didn't see the point in moving.'

She stood abruptly to leave. He braced himself for what was coming but, surprisingly, it never came.

'So we'll continue this conversation later then?' she asked, somewhat awkwardly.

It was his turn to blink. He was barely able to murmur a lame 'Yeah' before she scuttled away. When she was gone, he was left to wonder, which conversation would they be continuing?

Back in Bennie's office, Dana fidgeted in her seat. Her mind kept drifting back to Bob and the conversation they'd had in his office, the way she'd left it. There'd been something of the old days lingering in the air and she'd grabbed at it foolishly, without hesitation. Her carelessness should've made her uneasy, but nothing was as it should've been since the day she first arrived. At this point, her behavior was par for the course. She sighed. Sitting here over-thinking it would get her nowhere and there was still work to be done.

Like most, the malware in this case relied on network connectivity. And although it would take several hours, perhaps even a couple days, to make a more thorough assessment, there was no need to put off basic countermeasures. If Mr. Porter's system was not the only one affected, it would be better to know sooner rather than later.

She carefully summarized the more pertinent details of her findings in a brief report for the network staff, avoiding any discussion of the nature of the malware or the name of the affected user. It was necessary, however, to divulge some key information, such as the file name, the relevant port number, and the remote host's IP address, if they were to create an effective network signature. With any luck, Karen's staff would have the company's network devices updated to detect and prevent further malicious activity by close of business.

She thought about Bob and his impulse to distrust his own employees. It wasn't an overreaction. It was a slippery slope that couldn't be avoided. In a company of this size, everyone had a job to do—everyone knew their place. Any disruption to the normal routine would be disastrous, no matter how likely it may be that one of their own was involved.

There was a light knock at the door. Dana turn to see Ruby standing there with her little note pad in hand.

'Any luck with that IP address?' asked Dana.

Ruby grimaced. 'Not really. I found a record of it in the DHCP server but, unfortunately, it's associated with a computer name that doesn't actually exist.'

Dana sat up in her chair. 'Do you mean it doesn't physically exist or that it doesn't logically exist?'

'Either. It didn't show up in Active Directory or on any of the network diagrams and no one's ever heard of it.'

'Did you check the recycle bin in Active Directory? Maybe someone tried to delete it from the system when they figured out we were on to them.'

Ruby shook her head. 'I thought of that. There's no sign of it anywhere.'

'This is looking more like an inside job every minute,' said Dana, not sure whether to be impressed by it or annoyed.

Ruby's eyes widened. 'Do you really think so?'

Dana's eyebrow shot up. 'Don't you?'

Ruby said nothing. Dana didn't hold it against her. In a situation like this it was always easier to be the outsider looking in than it was to be the insider looking at the people around you.

'So it's a no-go with the IP address. I can live with that for now.' She handed Ruby a hard copy of the report for the network technicians. 'Be discrete about it but make the rounds and see what you can do with this. Let's leave the IP address in the mix for the time being and just see what happens.'

Ruby took the piece of paper, clearly unconvinced, before dutifully heading for the door. Dana smiled. She was going to make a security analyst out of that girl yet.

Alone again, Dana settled down with her laptop. She was ready to have a closer look at Mr. Porter's hard drive. In theory, every email he wrote, every scrap of document he edited, every password he entered since the keylogger was installed on his computer would be tucked away in a text file somewhere in the unallocated space where files go to die. It was a common misconception in the modern world that the word *delete* meant *destroy*. Nothing could be further from the truth. Files weren't destroyed, they were overwritten. And until that happened, they sat in their little space, completely unfazed by the whirlwind of activity around them.

It took some time in the initial setup but, eventually, she had a clear picture of everything that remained in the unallocated space of his hard drive. This space was technically up for grabs by any application that needed to write something to disk but, more often than not, most of it sat untouched—sometimes for years. That was certainly the case here. Just as Bob predicted, there was a long line of .txt files dating back to the 29th of April, nearly four months ago.

Tempting as it was to drill into some of those files, Dana simply made a note of the date and, instead, turned her attention to the printouts Ruby had given her the day before. It would be up to Bob to verify the contents of the files; in the meantime, she could establish the timeline and perhaps even narrow events down to their source.

She flipped through the pages, swearing at her own shortsightedness. She only requested 90 days worth of material. There were numerous complaints of various security-related incidents documented in the report, but there wasn't enough information to form any conclusions. In fact, the only thing of interest were the number of visits Bennie made to the offices of

Dean Forrester and Sam Porter during the last month. The latter was especially perplexing considering Mr. Porter just told her Bennie hadn't looked at his computer in quite some time.

She picked up the phone on Bennie's desk and dialed Ruby's number. She answered.

'Hey, it's me,' said Dana. 'When you get a chance, will you rerun the report you ran for me yesterday morning—only this time extend the search parameters to include everything from the last 12 months.'

Ruby made no comment but Dana sensed her surprise. 'Sure,' she said. 'I can have it for you by tomorrow morning.'

Dana thanked her and hung up the phone. She looked around the room, wishing Bennie had been a better note taker. But, then again, maybe he had been. She slid his notebook out of her bag and thumbed through the pages. There were bound to be answers in here.

She shoved the notebook back into her bag and reached for her laptop. She might be a little rusty but she could certainly write a program that could crack an antique cipher. How hard could it be?

Dana was silently kicking herself in the ass. How hard could it be to crack a Vigenère cipher? Pretty damn hard, apparently. Why didn't she just think to Google it?

It was too late for that now she thought as she carefully typed in a block of ciphertext from Bennie's notebook. She'd already gone through the trouble of using Python to teach the computer how to speak English. Or how *to detect* English, as the case may be. And then she spent the better part of three hours developing a programmatic method to derive the required encryption key using only the ciphertext before finally throwing together a function that would use the derived key to decrypt the jumbled mass into readable plaintext. It all hinged, of course, on whether her little program even worked—and whether his notes were in English.

She studied the block of text on the screen and compared it to the small print in the notebook:

PBZGJUNDPW

AFLAXYPDLW

WZRAOYFGPF

WOXRNIFSQM

LRJHDWGCDJ

BZCLQBCCPX

DCKBCYISYS

UGTUFXWVPE

HS

She hit the enter key and waited for the program to do something, crossing her fingers there would be no error messages. There weren't. Not only that, she hit pay dirt on her very first try.

PLAINTEXT:

INITIALTESTRUNWENTASPLANNEDWEBPAGEMODIFIED SUCCESSFULLYPHASETWOTOBEGINONSCHEDULEAAE

KEY:

HORNBUCKLE

She whistled. The empty room said nothing. Initial test run? Phase two? What the hell was Bennie into here? And what was *aae*? Dana pondered the question. Maybe they were numbers? If a = 1 and e = 5, then perhaps *aae* = 115. *Phase two to begin on schedule 115*... did he mean January 15th? And look at the key! Hornbuckle. As in Ruby Hornbuckle, her innocent, or perhaps *not* so innocent, assistant.

She checked the time on her phone. It was getting late, she was due to meet Bob in just over an hour. There was no way she could finish this tonight. She considered taking it with her but something prevented her from it. If he was being warned off by his superiors, handing the notebook over would just add fuel to the fire. Detective Mercer's advice was apt. She should play her cards close to the table for the time being.

But that didn't mean she was without allies. She had colleagues back at BDS who were always up for something out of the ordinary. And she might even be able to initiate a 'test run' of her own while she was at it.

She dialed the number for the lab. Eli answered.

She kept her voice low. 'Eli! I'm so glad you answered! Are you still covering for Alex?'

'For the rest of the week. What's up? And where are you? You sound far away.'

'I'm up to my neck in intrigue over here and I could really use your help.'

'Oh, *intrigue*,' he replied, lowering his own voice conspiratorially. 'What kind of intrigue?'

She could tell he was interested. 'I can't talk about it here. Mazie will have to explain it to you later.' She couldn't resist adding, 'I need a favor and I was sort of hoping the two of you could work on it together.'

Dana's skin was slick with moisture under her shirt. The sun was tracking downward in the sky but, without a breeze to push it along, the heat of the day hung in the air like smoke. She shifted the weight of her bag on her shoulder and shielded her eyes with one hand while fanning herself with the other until, finally, she spotted Mazie's SUV turning into the Grasslands parking lot.

Mazie came up beside her and cut the engine before hopping out. Her clothes clung to her body and the hair at the nape of her neck was damp. She looked uncomfortable to say the least.

'Okay, sister,' said Mazie, flipping her sunglasses up onto to the top of her head, 'spill it. Why did I just leave my job to come see you at yours in this infernal heat? It's quittin' time and my air-conditioned house is way the hell on the other side of town.'

Dana grinned. Mazie was adorable when she was fired up about something. 'I hate to tell you, sister, but it's even farther than that cuz you don't live in town. I need your help.'

Mazie snorted. 'And this explains why you chose for us to meet way out here, in the North 40? I'm pretty sure I drove by one of Jesus' shoes about a half a mile back.'

'Oh, hush. You're gonna love this, you just don't know it yet.' Dana reached into her bag and produced Bennie's notebook along with a copy of the decryption program burned to a CD. 'Eli's working the late shift and I need the two of you to decrypt these notes. It's the only thing we've got that might tell us what Bennie's really been up to.'

Mazie perked up visibly at the mention of Eli's name but even the prospect of an evening alone with him wasn't enough to stifle her curiosity. '*Decrypt these notes?* That sounds intriguing.' She held the notebook and CD slightly away from her as if holding them close would somehow make her hotter than she already was. 'Okay, but if Eli and I are doing this, what are you doing?'

Dana couldn't hide her blush. 'I have a late meeting.' She didn't say with whom. She didn't need to.

'With Bob,' Mazie surmised. Her eyes narrowed as she studied her friend's face. 'Are the two of you getting back together again?'

'What? How can you even ask that? No, we're not getting back together. This meeting is strictly professional.'

Mazie raised an eyebrow but said nothing. Dana was aware she was being defensive but couldn't do anything to stop it.

'You sound just like Floretta,' she said, suddenly exasperated. 'And, just like Floretta, you're *wrong*.'

'Whatever you say,' said Mazie, climbing back up into her vehicle to deposit the notebook and CD into the passenger seat. She looked at herself in the rear view mirror and fluffed her hair, obviously disgusted by what she saw. 'Well, it's a good thing Eli already knows what I look like,' she declared, somewhat ruefully.

Dana looked up at her beautiful friend of many years, trying to remember when she'd become so insecure about her appearance. Time could be so cruel. People could be so cruel. Dana had grown up in the city, near a college campus, the daughter of two professors, but her mother routinely dragged her off to the country to visit Tillie. If she closed her eyes, she could still hear the voices of the two women locked in earnest debate about the precise translation of something or other. For Dana, it was all sheer boredom until, one day, a pudgy little girl came bouncing onto the scene, courtesy of Mrs. Reid, with her red cheeks and her sharp wit and her miles and miles of imagination. It was friendship at first sight. How they looked was never part of the equation back then.

Dana smiled at the memory. 'You're much prettier than you think you are, Mazie Reid. And Eli's a lot more into you than you think, too, so go have some fun.'

Mazie smiled and fired up the engine, popping her sunglasses back on her face. She turned the AC up to full blast and made sure all the vents were pointed directly at her.

'You, too,' she called over the rushing air. 'And make sure you call me first thing in the morning, I want to hear every juicy detail.'

Dana laughed and waved goodbye as she headed to her own vehicle, grateful to be meeting with Bob away from the gray, confined spaces of GES, even if it was at his private residence. It wasn't until she was busy angling her own vents in pursuit of cold air that it occurred to her. She'd forgotten to tell Mazie about the offer letter that was still in her bag, unsigned. Gossip traveled faster than the speed of light at BDS—if Mazie heard about it from someone else, Dana would never hear the end of it.

Bob was an old-fashioned guy. *You pick out the house*, he'd said, *and I'll pay for it.* And so it was that she found herself in harrowing traffic at 6:40 PM, en route to the house she'd chosen because of its proximity to, well, *everything*. It was an older neighborhood but the homes here were still immaculately maintained, almost in defiance of the roadways and parking lots that threatened to encroach from outside. The noise of civilization was somewhat muffled by the trees and the shrubs and the fences but it was nothing like the quiet of the country. It was amazing to think she'd ever thought she would raise a family here.

The ranch-style house looked the same as ever except for a new carport over the driveway and a long, gently-sloping ramp that eased up to the now-wider front door. A minivan was parked under the shade of the carport and Dana realized it must be his vehicle. She hadn't thought of him driving but it made sense that he would. The man was independent to a fault.

Seconds after she rang the bell, the door swung wide. Bob was sitting there in his chair, his shirtsleeves rolled up to his forearms, blue eyes glinting, smiling his strange little smile. He almost seemed surprised to see her standing there. He probably didn't think she'd have the guts to show. It occurred to her that neither one of them knew how much the other had changed in the past four years. They were in new territory.

'I'm glad you decided to come,' he said, almost boyishly, as he wheeled back and waved her in. 'I hope you don't mind but I went ahead and made something for us to eat. I just need to finish setting the kitchen table.'

She followed him to the kitchen, absorbing details of the house as she went. The carpeting had been replaced with wood laminate, the doorways were wider, and several of the cabinets and counters had been lowered but, for the most part, it was the same. It was clean and well-furnished. Downright cozy.

'You cooked?'

'Don't sound so surprised. I've learned a thing or two about this whole cooking thing.' He wheeled up to a low counter and lifted the lid on a slow cooker. The smell of roast with gravy and vegetables wafted up into the air. It looked incredible. 'I especially like this whole Crock Pot business. All I have to do is put the stuff in and turn it on.'

She was too stunned to say anything. Her mind raced; she could actually hear Floretta's voice pounding away in her ears. Suddenly feeling woozy and over-warm, she frantically searched for a chair. She needed air, lots of cold air, and something to sit on.

Bob must have seen the look on her face because he rushed over and grabbed her before she had a chance to slide to the floor. She teetered on his lap momentarily before he grabbed hold of her and wheeled them both carefully down the hallway to the master bedroom where he deposited her on the bed and took himself into the bathroom. A few moments later, he resurfaced with a cool washcloth for her face, which she accepted before retreating into the comfort of the bed.

He slid her shoes off and casually began messaging one of her feet like he used to. 'So what's this about? Is my cooking really that bad?' he teased gently.

She looked at him. 'You're better,' she said simply.

His hands froze. He looked at her, obviously unsure how to respond so he just waited for her to say something instead.

'You live in this house, alone, and you've made it beautiful. All by yourself.' Her voice trailed off. 'You clean. You drive. You cook. You've healed. You've moved on.' Her voice dropped to a whisper. 'You're better. You're better without me.'

Bob studied her face and then resumed with the foot massage. 'Yes, well, looks can be deceiving, can't they?'

She stirred. He smiled. 'Now don't get me wrong, I am doing well. I am, as you say, *better*, but it took a lot work to get this far. I only started cooking when I couldn't stand the taste of peanut butter anymore and, even then, it was hit or miss. Mostly miss. And you really don't want to know how many times I fell on my ass trying to make this chair do something it didn't want to do. Truth be known, I'm lucky as hell I didn't break my back a second time. But you get up and then you get up again and, eventually, you learn how to make your way.'

Finished with one foot, he grabbed the other and laughed at some thought in his own head. 'It's ironic. Here you are thinkin' I've been better off without you when the only reason I've been without you is because I thought you'd be better off without me.'

Dana sat up, still holding the damp cloth to her forehead. 'I thought you said you were running from something.'

He shrugged. 'I was. I was running from the life of an invalid. You bathed me, you fed me, you changed me, you smothered me with love and concern—'

'What's wrong with that?' she demanded. 'What's wrong with any of those things? I did love you, I *was* concerned—'

'You deserved better. And so did I.' He swore and raked his

hand through his hair. 'Everyone kept telling me it would get better but it just kept getting worse. Everyone kept saying, '*this too shall pass,*' as if they knew what they were talking about. But the truth was we were never gonna be free of it.'

'So you made the decision for both of us.' Her voice sounded hollow, even to her. How could he do that to her, knowing her as well as he did?

Dana dropped the wet cloth and dragged her shoes on her feet. 'You had no right to shut me out, Bob Leroy. I have as much right to grieve as you do.'

She launched herself off the bed in the direction of the door but he reached out with his long, powerful arms to stop her. He pulled her back into his lap and leaned in, his forehead firmly against hers. 'I am not your father and I did not do to you what your father did to you.' She let out a sob but he kept talking. 'I can't take back what happened. And I can't go back there, to that night—not even with you. You understand that, right? I can't go backwards, I have to move forward.' He sucked in a breath. 'And I think you should, too.'

She felt him release her but she stayed, sitting limply like a tired child, unsure of what came next. All her anger, all her fear, all her hurt, so intense five seconds ago, began sliding into memory. It was all still there but, somehow, less vivid.

'I'll tell you what,' he said softly. He retrieved the cool cloth and pressed it on the back of her neck. 'Why don't you stay in here for a spell, freshen up and do whatever it is you ladies do, and then we can have dinner and talk about anything you want.'

She thought about that for a minute and finally decided she had nothing to lose. 'Fine, but—just so we're clear—we're not having sex.'

Having dealt with her appearance, Dana hung the wet washcloth on a towel rack to dry and followed the aroma of food into the kitchen where Bob was busy laying out butter and a plate of sliced bread. Her mouth watered at the sight of the thick cuts of beef, attractively arranged and poised to break apart perfectly. There wasn't much in this world that could diminish her appetite. Despite everything, she was famished.

'I hope you're hungry,' said Bob as he held a chair back from the table for her.

She nodded and slid into the offered seat. It was the same dinette set he'd had in his apartment when they first met, the perfect size for a kitchen. There was already a glass of iced tea set at her place at the table, which she gulped greedily. It was cold and sweet, just the way she liked it. It was refreshing and energizing at the same time.

Bob grabbed the pitcher of tea off a low counter and refilled her glass while she generously loaded her plate. 'I take it you're feeling better?' he teased with a smile.

She forked a tender carrot, enjoying the meal too much to be embarrassed. 'I am, thank you.' She savored the taste of the carrot, soft and slightly sweet, before continuing. 'I guess I was less prepared for this encounter than I thought.'

Bob loaded an equally generous serving of meat and vegetables onto his own plate before looking across at her. 'Me too, but I'm glad you're here all the same.'

She smiled but said nothing. They settled into amicable silence as they ate. She was reminded of her mother, who used to say that nothing in life was so bad it couldn't be fixed with a good meal, a hot bath, and clean sheets. It was apt advice.

She looked up from her empty plate to see Bob using a large piece of bread to sop up the last of his gravy. It was impossible to hide her amusement when he proceeded to fold it up, quite ceremoniously, and cram the whole thing into his mouth.

He noticed her expression and swallowed hard before asking, 'What are you smiling at?'

She grinned. 'I was just thinking that some things never change, no matter what goes on around them.'

His response was tentative. 'Is that a good thing?'

'It's a good thing.'

She looked back down at her empty plate with sadness. Would it be rude to go for seconds on the potatoes? She was contemplating this very important question when Bob's rolling, baritone laughter suddenly filled the room. His eyes were twinkling.

'How about some dessert?' he asked.

All thoughts of potatoes flew out of her brain. 'You made dessert?'

He shrugged. 'Sort of. We're having strawberries.'

'Sprinkled with sugar?'

'Is there any other way?' he asked as he wheeled over to the fridge.

'With whipped cream?'

'Out of a can but, yes, with whipped cream.'

He returned to the table with two bowls of strawberries, glazed with their own juices, and a can of whipped cream.

'Do you remember the strawberry cake we got from that fancy bakery for your birthday a few years back?' he asked, setting one of the bowls down in front of her.

She smiled at the memory. 'How could I forget? We had to serve it in the bathroom because the tornado sirens kept going off.'

'And when the cake ran out, we all got drunk on Mrs. Reid's homemade strawberry wine.' He swirled whipped cream high in his bowl. 'Isn't that the same night you told me that we might have to sacrifice our lives for our guests?'

'Well, we couldn't *all* fit into the bathtub now could we?' she said in mock defense. 'Can you imagine what would've happened if we left them to die and then they *didn't* die?'

'I think Mazie would have taken it the hardest,' replied Bob, matter-of-factly, around a mouthful of berries.

She smiled at that and wondered how Mazie and Eli were faring with Bennie's notebook. Sitting there, eating a bowl of fruit, Bob looked more like a corn-fed farm hand than a senior executive at an energy company. She would tell him about the notebook, she decided, as soon as she knew what they were dealing with. There was no point in getting bogged down in something that was all questions and no answers.

'So how are things at Bellwether?' asked Bob, dragging her out of her thoughts.

Dana blinked, catching up to the question. 'I got a promotion,' she blurted.

His eyes widened and she felt herself blush.

'I mean, technically it's just an offer. I haven't signed it or anything. At least not yet. I haven't actually spoken to Jeremy about it yet, either,' she rambled on, 'or Floretta, come to think of it. Or Mazie.'

She fell silent as Bob digested the news.

'So this is all a good thing, right?' he asked.

'Of course. I mean, it's mostly a good thing. I think.' She shrank in her chair and absently fiddled with the ring beneath her shirt that hung from the chain around her neck. She finally settled on the truth. 'It's complicated.'

He'd noticed her fiddling. She could see the curiosity etched on his face but he said nothing.

'So how about you?' she asked. 'Do you like it at Grasslands?'

There was a pause before he spoke. 'Not really. Don't get me wrong,' he added hastily, 'it's a good job. Great pay, good benefits, all that. In this economy, I'm damn lucky and I know it. But the work itself,' he trailed off, searching for the words. 'Well, it's like going into battle—every single day of my working life.'

'Is Karen that much of an obstacle?'

'Karen?' He shook his head. 'She's the least of my worries. My problems can all be reduced to numbers.' He chuckled. 'You like numbers, maybe they should've hired you as their CIO.'

'What kind of numbers are we talking about?'

'Return on Investment, quantitative risk assessments, pretty much anything you can think of that's used to justify why it isn't cost-effective to do the right thing.'

'I don't know much about that. I majored in math, not business.'

'And I majored in computer science so I guess neither of us is qualified for the job.' He sagged into his chair. 'I'm dealing with a bunch of good ol' boys that only respond to discrete concepts reduced to figures on a page that have more in common with abstract art than reality. They base their information security decisions on best-guess percentages using the most unimaginative scenarios and then debate how likely one thing is over another, despite the fact that we live in a world where all things are possible. It's horrible.'

She could sympathize. 'Surely there's a way. I mean, they have to come to terms eventually. They don't call it the Information Age for nothing.'

Bob sat up straighter and took a sip of his tea. 'I have a plan. Or, at least, I *did* have a plan. With Bennie gone, I really don't know how things are going to turn out. Maybe this thing with Sam's system will be the thing that motivates them.'

Having eaten her strawberries, Dana pushed her empty bowl aside and glanced at the cheerful clock hanging on the wall. It was getting late. She collected the dishes and took them to the sink but he wouldn't hear of her washing anything. He insisted that she was a guest and, therefore, shouldn't have to wash dishes, even if she could be comfortably seated in a chair the whole time.

Instead, she let him walk her out to her car where they said their goodbyes. He surprised her by taking her hand and pressing a kiss on the inside of her wrist. Her skin tingled where his lips had been even after she pulled out of the driveway. He'd never kissed her there before.

She dug her Bluetooth headset out of the cup holder that was never used for cups and voice-dialed Mazie. She answered on the first ring.

'I had a feelin' you were gonna call, my left ear was itchin'. How'd it go with Bob?'

Dana smiled in the darkness. 'It was good. How'd it go with Eli?'

There was a brief pause. 'It was good.'

Dana chuckled inwardly. If Mazie's tone was anything to go by, it was better than good.

'Did he ask you out?' she asked.

'Is it that obvious?'

'Yes.'

'Well, then, yes, he asked me out.'

'And did you say yes?'

'Did I say yes? Are you kidding? When a gorgeous, brilliant, single, totally sane man asks you out to dinner, of course you say yes. Everyone knows this.'

'So how did it go with the notebook?'

'Ah, well, we finished the decryption. Eli had to tweak your program a bit to handle the numbers but, other than that, it worked perfectly.'

'And?'

There was another pause, longer this time. Finally, she spoke. 'You have a problem.'

CHAPTER SIX

Of Course It's Latin

The sun pierced through the slats of the vertical window blinds in Bennie's office, creating thin yellow-gold ribbons that stretched the length of the room, straight across the desk and over the decrypted text of Bennie's notebook that Dana had been pouring over for the last two hours. The light spilling across the pages barely registered in her mind, however, as the full force of her thoughts were focused on the text underneath.

She struggled for perspective. She'd been brought here to investigate the circumstances of Bennie's death; instead, her one and only piece of evidence turned out to be a detailed account of his crimes.

There was only one thing to do. Dana picked up the phone and dialed Ruby's number. She needed to narrow the playing field and Ruby was the key, literally. It was a risky move. If Ruby was involved, she was in a position to interfere but it couldn't be helped.

Despite the early hour, Ruby answered on the first ring.

'Hey, it's me,' said Dana, adopting what she hoped was an unsuspecting demeanor. 'I was wondering if you had a chance to print that report I requested yesterday?'

There was a brief pause, followed by vigorous typing and the sound of a printer warming up in the background.

'I'll have it for you in five minutes,' said Ruby, giving no indication that she was anything less than prepared. She was a hard worker, Dana had to give her that.

True to her word, Ruby showed up a few minutes later with a stack of printed pages much thicker than the previous set. Dana accepted them eagerly.

'Thank you for these,' she said, keeping her tone light. 'I ran across some of Bennie's notes and I'm struggling to understand them—he seems to have developed his own particular shorthand. I decided it might be helpful to compare them to what's recorded in the trouble ticket system.'

She watched Ruby's face carefully but detected no change, no hint of recognition or concern. For her part, Ruby simply nodded. Dana pressed on.

'He noted a number of incidents stretching back as far as January and I'm wondering if any them might be related to what we discovered yesterday morning.'

Ruby's response to this was only of slight confusion, nothing more.

'I can go back as far as you want but didn't you say the malware was created in April?'

Dana nodded. 'I did. But it's always possible the attacker made multiple attempts before they found a way to make it work. It can be just as much trial and error for them as it is for us.'

To this, Ruby simply nodded again. No stammering, no blushing. Dana took it as evidence that Ruby knew nothing of Bennie's activities. She had to acknowledge the possibility that he used Ruby's name simply because it was easy to remember but difficult to guess, while also being long enough for his purposes. The fact that each letter appeared only once was probably just icing on the cake. It wasn't meant to be unbreakable but, rather, breakable in the right hands. The question that filled her mind was whether the notes were for his own use or if they were meant to be some kind of insurance policy. If the latter, there was bound to be at least two other actors in play: one who was meant to retrieve the notebook and decipher its contents and another who would be threatened by its existence. But who was who?

She shook her head. In all likelihood, she would never know the answers. But that didn't mean she couldn't rule someone out and Ruby just didn't fit the bill. This line of inquiry was over.

'When you get a chance,' said Dana, electing to steer the conversation elsewhere, 'check in with the network team and see if our little malware friend has generated any alerts since yesterday.'

'I'm pretty sure they beat us to it but I can't find anything out until they leave Karen's office.'

Dana quirked an eyebrow. 'They're in with Karen? Right now?'

'Yeah, the firewall guy is in there with his supervisor and a couple of other guys from the same section. They don't usually come in this early and you hardly ever see them out here, where the rest of us are, so something has to be going on.'

Dana agreed. If the recluses were coming out of the woodwork, something was definitely up. 'Good to know. Go see what you can find out and get back to me.'

When Ruby left, Dana closed the door behind her. She eyed the stacks of papers on the desk with a grimace. Her plan was to divide and conquer, her weapon of choice was a yellow highlighter. It was an arduous task. One by one, she compared the entries from Bennie's notebook to the printed report of past trouble tickets submitted by GES employees. The resulting image was painfully clear. The notebook contained detailed accounts of incidents that were not actually reported to the help desk for anywhere from one to several days after the date of the entry.

Even more incriminating were the dates indicating when something was expected to occur, as was the case with the very first entry. Although he didn't date the entry itself, he mentioned another date that correlated to an incident reported to the help desk in the same time frame. The only reasonable conclusion was that he had prior knowledge of these events because he perpetrated them. What wasn't clear was why. The incidents themselves were all but harmless, easy to identify and easy to fix. If there was a pattern, or a purpose, it wasn't obvious.

The only entries in the notebook that did not directly correlate to an event between the first of the year and two weeks before Bennie's death were a series of tables and notes that made no sense out of context. They were so wildly different from everything that came before them that she wondered if they weren't notes describing something still in the planning stages but, if that was the case, where were the plans for all the others?

One thing was certain, though. Whatever game Bennie was playing at, he was willing to risk his career and, whether he knew it or not, his life. Corporate America was not without its dirty little secrets. Acts of treason did not go unnoticed and not all roads were high roads.

Her mind kept returning to the problem at hand, Mr. Porter's system. Nothing in the notebook suggested a connection but that didn't mean there wasn't one. None of his previous exploits included anything as complicated as homespun malware, let alone something sophisticated enough to avoid detection for any period of time. That being the case, was Bennie so wrapped up in his own shenanigans that he simply overlooked the real threat affecting his network or did he purposely ignore it?

She gathered all the papers into a pile and slid them into her bag. She needed to talk to Bob about this immediately. She barely had her cell phone in hand when the door flew open, revealing an outraged Karen. Dana was momentarily taken aback by the sheer volume of anger rolling her way.

Karen marched into the room like a soldier and spoke with the command of a general. Her voice was pure poison.

'I don't appreciate being blindsided by my employees, Ms. Sorensen. I especially don't appreciate having to tap dance my way through an issue without any background information to go on. Now you may not work for me but you're for damn sure not the superior in this relationship so I'd like to know when, exactly, you were planning to tell me about this creptio bullshit.'

'Creptio?' asked Dana, genuinely mystified.

Karen's tone turned to disgust. 'If you don't recognize Latin when you see it, there's nothing I can do for you. Now answer my damn question.'

Dana prayed for tact. 'Since Mr. Leroy engaged my services, my company recognizes him as the client. In accordance with our policy, I visited with him briefly yesterday afternoon to explain my findings, which are, frankly, incomplete at this time. I had Ruby share what information we had with your network team as a basic precaution while I continue my analysis, which is standard procedure with malware.'

'How nice,' Karen seethed. 'A canned response. And so *professional.*' She stalked over to the only unoccupied chair in the room and sat down, crossing her legs elegantly. 'Well, you'll be happy to know your incomplete information resulted in more alerts than I can count. And if we believe these results, nearly every senior executive in this company is affected. Unfortunately, I don't have a choice but to respond—not just to respond but to respond *in a big way*—so here's what we're gonna do. You, personally, are going to run this thing to ground. As of this moment, it's your only priority. And there will be no more Ruby. If you need anything from my people, you will go through me.'

Karen stood and crossed the room like a huntress until she towered over Dana's seated frame. 'Now, if you were too hasty with your incomplete information—if you're *wrong*—then just know that I will hang you out to dry.'

'Which executives aren't affected?'

Karen blinked. 'What?'

'You said nearly every senior executive is affected so I was just wondering which ones weren't.'

Karen's reply was curt. 'The only C-level executive who isn't on the list is Bob Leroy, along with most of the department heads. But you should already know that, shouldn't you? It is your job, after all.'

Karen exited with a flourish, leaving Dana alone to stew in the stinging venom that still hung in the air. Karen did give her an idea, though. She looked at her cell phone, still in her hand, and called Mazie.

'Hey girl! Are we doing lunch?'

'I don't think I can swing it today but that's not why I'm calling, anyway. Have you ever heard of the word creptio?'

'Creptio?'

'It's Latin.'

'Of course it's Latin.'

Dana closed her eyes, wondering when the whole direct question, direct answer thing went out of style. 'Yes, but what does it *mean*?'

'It has more than one meaning but the most common is seizure. You know, taking something by force.' Mazie's voice turned suspicious. 'Why? Have you seen this word somewhere?'

Dana grabbed a piece of scrap paper off the desk and wrote out the name of the executable she'd found on Mr. Porter's computer, minus the extension: CRE_pt10.

'As a matter of fact,' she said. 'I believe I have.'

Bob checked his watch. Almost twenty-four hours without a pill and still going strong, not that he would've noticed if he weren't. After last night, he could think of nothing but Dana. The way her body felt as he held her, the smell of her hair, how she said a dozen things without so much as a single word. She satisfied a craving he didn't even realize he had and, now that she was back in his life, he wouldn't let her go again without a fight.

There was a rap at the door before Helen popped her head in. 'Ms. Sorensen is here to see you. Would you like me to send her in?'

Speakin' of the devil. He sat up as tall as he could in his chair and straightened his tie. 'By all means, send her in.'

Helen smiled a knowing little smile as she backed out of the room and opened the door wide enough for Dana to slip in before closing it behind her. Bob's mouth went dry. No matter how hard she tried to hide it, Dana was just as curvy as she was petite and he recalled the feel of those curves all too well.

'We need to talk,' she said, helping herself to a chair across from him. Her tone was serious, too serious.

His stomach clenched. He could actually feel his chest deflating. He should've known she'd have second thoughts. 'Yeah, about last night—'

'I'm not here about last night.' A look of concern flitted across her face. 'Why? Do we need to talk about last night?'

He sat dumbfounded, struggling to comprehend. 'No,' he said

at last. 'I mean, we can talk about it if you want but I thought it was good.' He couldn't resist adding, 'Didn't you think it was good?'

A smile played on her lips. 'It was good. But that's not what I came here to talk about.'

Relieved, he leaned back in his chair. 'I'm all ears.'

'It's about Bennie,' she said as she rifled through the bag at her feet. She emerged with a notebook, marred by broad pieces of tape, and placed it on his desk.

He recognized it immediately. It would be impossible not to since there were several examples of it locked away in his desk at that very moment. He would've sworn he'd recovered them all but, apparently, he did not.

He punted. 'What's this?'

'I found it strapped under Bennie's desk. It's encrypted.'

Bob picked up the notebook and turned the pages, frankly confused. Bennie was a prodigious note-taker but the agreement had been to document everything as though they were incidents currently under review, regardless of their actual status, to avoid suspicion. Unless you knew what you were looking at, the notes were completely innocuous. In fact, if not for Dean's prying, he never would've had to take them out of Bennie's office in the first place. But this? This was something else altogether.

'I assume you decrypted it?'

'I had a helluva time, let me tell you. I wrote the program but I had Mazie and Eli do the rest,' she explained. 'They emailed me the plaintext last night.' She scooted forward in the chair and dropped her voice to a whisper. 'I compared these entries to your internal records and it's plain as day. Bennie was manufacturing incidents at this company and passing them off as real. What I don't know is why. And I'm inclined to think someone figured out what he was up to and either found a way to retaliate or just plain scared him so bad that he really did take his own life.' She sat up suddenly, apparently struck by an idea. 'He was an anxious sort, right? If there *was* a confrontation, maybe he was just looking for a fast way to calm his nerves and made a fatal miscalculation.'

Bob closed his eyes. Christ, but this was going off the rails. Bennie Price did not die of an accidental overdose, nor did he commit suicide. He had to tell her, even if it meant pushing her further away. His brain seized at the thought. The dragon in his head stirred. His migraine meds were in the top drawer of his desk but it was too late. If it started breathing fire now, the drugs would never get into his bloodstream fast enough.

'Bennie's death has nothing to do with this notebook,' he announced, keeping his voice quiet. He closed the book and firmly pushed it back across the desk in her direction. 'And I know that because his actions were sanctioned. By me.'

She sat bolt upright in the chair, a circus of emotions playing out on her face. Her initial skepticism rapidly changed from confusion to comprehension to anger.

'*This* was your plan?' It was more of an accusation than a question. '*This* was your big ploy to get the funding you needed? To get them to care?'

He squared his shoulders and spoke plainly. 'Yes.'

She sputtered and swore violently, her words barely intelligible. Finally, she heaved in a breath and narrowed her eyes at him. 'Why didn't you tell me?' she demanded. 'You should've told me about this when I first got here. Barring that, you sure as hell should've told me last night.'

She stood up and began pacing a hole into his carpet. He wished to hell he could join her.

'I didn't want to drag you into my mess.'

She spun around to face him. 'I am sick to death of people making decisions for me, Bob Leroy,' she hissed. 'Sick. To. Death. Now either we're in this together or we aren't. Telling lies and withholding information never saved anyone from the harsh realities of life so, if you don't mind, I'd like to know what the hell is going on here so I can make up my own damn mind.'

Dana threw herself down in the chair and crossed her arms expectantly. He knew full well that any attempt to unruffle her feathers would end in disaster. This chickadee did not like to be handled. Honesty was the only option.

He drug in a breath. 'Like you said, this was the plan. Bennie and I cooked it up late last year after it became clear that our proposal for much-needed improvements would not be included in this year's budget. Our ideas were deemed *cost-ineffective*. So we thought, what the hell? If they want to play with fire, let 'em see what it's like to feel the flames.'

She was incredulous. 'So you decided *to spy* on the senior management of your own company?'

Bob sat up, frankly offended by the insinuation. 'We staged a series of mostly-harmless, controlled attacks designed to get their attention, nothing more. Not exactly the pinnacle of ethical standards but hardly criminal.'

'Well that depends on who you ask now doesn't it?' she quipped.

'What's that supposed to mean?' he growled. He may be in love with her but that didn't make the idea of showing her the door any less appealing.

'It means that a backdoor with an embedded keylogger is currently residing on computers belonging to every C-level executive in this building except yours. You expect me to believe that's a coincidence?'

He blinked. He felt the sting of her words as strongly as if she'd slapped him. She didn't believe him. More than that, he wasn't sure if she should believe him. He eyed the notebook resting on the far side of the desk. He hadn't read the plaintext. Maybe she knew something he didn't.

'I have no knowledge of any backdoors or keyloggers on this network and that's the truth. Bennie and I never discussed anything like that. Now, if you're telling me you found something in that notebook—'

'The notebook makes no mention of malware,' she admitted, 'but that doesn't mean there isn't a connection. It'll all come out eventually so you might as well come clean now. It'll save us both a lot of trouble in the end.'

'I'm not lying,' he spat, his anger rising. 'I'm not aware of any connection and that's all there is to it.'

She studied his face, obviously at war with herself. He didn't feel inclined to make it any easier for her. If she knew him as well as she should, then she'd know he didn't have the appetite for espionage. He didn't expect her to trust him but she should damn sure know what he was and was not capable of. They were almost married for Christ's sakes.

'Well, then, how can you be so sure someone else didn't find out what you were up to?' she asked finally.

Bob swore. It was a good question, one that he didn't have a good answer for. 'Someone did know,' he admitted. 'Dean Forrester knew, he just couldn't prove it.'

Dana screwed up her face. 'The CEO? How did he figure it out before anyone else?'

'My question exactly. I assume someone tipped him off but, whoever that person was, they had no proof. Not that Dean needs proof. If it weren't for Sam intervening on Bennie's behalf, Bennie would've been fired weeks ago.'

'How did you manage to escape the hot seat?' The accusatory tone was back.

'My name never came up so I have to assume the tipster knew nothing of my involvement. It turned out to be a good thing, too, because Sam handed the internal investigation over to me.'

'So, what, you were just going to wait an appropriate amount of time and declare the accusation unfounded?'

'Yes, actually, that was the plan. But I couldn't make it stick. Sam figured out I was protecting Bennie and put a stop to it. I bought Bennie some time but that was the best I could do. Sam and I agreed, however, that Bennie could resign. And then Floretta was prepared to offer him a position back at Bellwether making more than he earned here and he was happy with the arrangement. So, you see, no one had any kind of motive to do anything to Bennie—'

'Because he was already on his way out,' she finished. 'He was leaving quietly. So what about you?'

He shrugged. 'My resignation letter is already drafted. The only reason I'm here now is to find out whatever it is that Bennie discovered. It's the key to his death—I'm sure of it—and, if something sinister is going on at this company, Sam deserves to know. He's been good to me, I owe him that much.'

Another rap at the door. It was Helen again. 'I'm sorry to disturb you but Grace just called. Mr. Porter is on his way down.'

Bob smiled ruefully. His head throbbed. Could his luck get any better? 'Thank you, Helen. See if you can stall him a minute, will you?'

When Helen disappeared through the door, he looked at Dana. 'So what are you gonna do?' he asked, aware that the ball was in her court.

She hesitated before answering. 'I'm going to give you the benefit of the doubt' she said finally. 'For now. But you should know you're on a short leash. If I find out that you and your boy were behind this, I will not hesitate to do my job.'

'How does that work if I'm the client?' he baited.

'You're not the client,' she replied. 'Not anymore. Now you're a suspect.'

Bob was a suspect. Dana could hardly believe her own words but it was true. She should've known he'd take matters into his own hands. Still, it was unlike him to let things get so out of control. She wanted to believe what he was saying but, if she was honest with herself, the evidence was stacked against him. It didn't matter how she felt, feelings couldn't be trusted. She had to use her brain and her brain dictated that nothing in this case was certain. She had to proceed carefully.

Mr. Porter's voice could be heard on the other side of the door. Helen's stall tactics were apparently futile against the round little man so prone to impatience. Dana straightened herself and noticed that Bob did the same. A deal had been struck. No matter what her misgivings, she would keep his secret as long as possible.

Mr. Porter pried open the door and bustled in, waving Helen away as though she were a bumble bee threatening to land on his picnic lunch. 'I don't care if he's in a meeting,' he snapped. 'I am the president of this god-forsaken company and I'll not be told—'

'Come on in Sam,' called Bob from his desk. Dana noticed he threw a placating look Helen's way, his version of an apology. Helen, it turned out, was not so easy to please.

No sooner had Helen retreated than Mr. Porter shut the door on her back with a resolute click. He turned to face them, his ruddy complexion shining under the fluorescent lights.

'I'm so glad I could catch the two of you at the same time,' he heaved. 'I just got a call from Dean. Karen's raisin' hell, turning the whole place on its head. I sure hope the two of you have a plan.'

Bob offered Sam a seat and picked up his phone. Dana could hear him quietly requesting a glass of cold water for his unexpected guest, quickly followed by his insistence that Helen should feel free to take the afternoon off at his expense. Moments later, Helen reappeared with the water, somewhat mollified, and Mr. Porter proceeded to drink heavily from the glass, apparently oblivious to any injury he might have caused.

'We were just discussing the way forward,' said Bob, pointedly looking at Dana. 'Weren't we?'

Dana nodded in agreement. 'Yes, we were just discussing the fact that we need to find the source of the malware.'

Mr. Porter huffed. 'The source? Why can't you just remove the damn thing and be done with it?'

'Well, we'll do that, too,' she acknowledged, 'but considering that such a small group of people are affected, and a select group of people at that, we really do need to root out the source.'

'I agree,' said Bob. 'The last thing we want is for someone to inadvertently reinfect their system.'

'So how do you figure on finding the source?'

'Well, I've been thinking about that,' said Dana, choosing her words carefully. 'We need to look for something that the affected users have in common with each other that they don't also have in common with everyone else.'

Mr. Porter nodded his head. 'I like it, in principle, but the only things the executives have in common are those things that are used by all of us, including Bob, and Karen says there's nothing wrong with his computer.'

'I can think of one thing we don't have in common,' offered Bob as he grabbed his mouse and began clicking. 'Financial reports.'

'Don't be ridiculous,' rebuked Mr. Porter. 'You get copied on financial reports the same as anybody else.'

'I get the reports,' corrected Bob, 'but I don't open them. My budget is practically non-existent, remember? And Larry holds a marathon budget meeting every other week just to rub it in. The reports are pointless.'

'Larry sends those reports out personally,' insisted Mr. Porter. 'He's been sending them out for years and there's never been a problem.'

Dana stood to make her way around the other side of the desk where Bob's email application was open on the desktop. He wasn't kidding about the financial reports. There were at least two years worth of emails parked in a subfolder that probably never saw the light of day. Same sender, same subject, all with attachments, all unread.

'There's no shame in digital signatures, you know,' she muttered for Bob's ears only. 'Or encryption.'

'Secure email costs money,' he muttered back. 'Do you have any to spare?'

She smiled in spite of herself. Grasslands really was behind the times. No wonder Bob resorted to fakery. At least it was one step above outright sabotage. If he was telling the truth, that is.

'I assume Larry works in finance?' she asked no one in

particular.

Mr. Porter nodded. 'Larry Katz. He's a department head, reports to the CFO. Been with the company more than twenty years. He's a good man.'

Dana scanned the emails for all dates in April of this year. 'And how often does he send these reports?'

'Once a week, usually on Monday,' supplied Mr. Porter. 'Why?'

'Is it unusual for him to send out multiple reports in one day?'

'There's no need to. It's just one report.'

Dana leaned over Bob's shoulder and used her finger to double-check the count. She hadn't made a mistake. 'April 28,' she said. 'I see two emails from Lawrence H. Katz, same subject, same day, one at 9:05 AM and the other at 10:36 AM.' She looked at Mr. Porter. 'How good is your memory?'

'There's a faster way,' said Bob, picking up the phone, dialing a number. Within seconds, he was locked in conversation with one Larry Katz. They spoke for several minutes but the shorthand communication between colleagues was impossible to follow. Mr. Porter was apparently having the same problem. He nearly fell out of his chair twice.

Bob hung up. Mr. Porter leaned forward expectantly, gripping the arms of the chair for stability. 'Out with it boy, what did he say?'

'He said he only sent one email on the 28th of April with that subject heading. Timestamp 9:05 AM.'

Mr. Porter swore. 'So who the hell sent the one at 10:36?'

'There's only way to find out,' said Bob, selecting the message.

Dana put her hand on his arm. 'Wait, you should change your settings so that it opens in plain text. Just in case.'

Bob nodded and made the change while Mr. Porter fidgeted. If the message was the source of the malware, they'd probably find it buried somewhere in the attachment, which meant nothing would happen until they opened the file. But HTML and Rich Text were perfectly viable means of transmission, too. If the attacker happened to take that route, Bob's computer would be at risk the second he double-clicked the message.

Mr. Porter was impatient. 'Well, who does it say it's from?'

'It says it's from Lawrence H. Katz,' replied Dana. 'But that's an easy thing to fake. The header information should tell us where the message originated.'

She watched over Bob's shoulder as he pulled up the Internet header that contained all the network information associated with the message. Where it came from, where it was going, which servers it passed through to get from one place to another. Technically speaking, everything in an email header could be forged but some things were more of a pain in the ass to monkey around with than others and so were less likely to be tampered with.

Bob pointed to the Received header section. 'I think we just found our answer.'

He was right. The IP address of the sender was definitely not a GES address. Larry Katz had been spoofed. She went back around the desk to where her bag was and entered the IP address into a

Whois lookup site using her cell phone. The result was not promising. 'Dead end. The IP address traces back to a commercial Internet Service Provider.'

'Why is that a dead end?' asked Mr. Porter. 'Can't you just call them?'

Bob shook his head. 'We can submit the request but they won't give us anything.'

Dana dug a thumb drive out of her bag. 'Bob's right,' she agreed. 'An ISP won't hand over anything without a court order. But at least we can use the information to set up a sniffer on the network.' She handed the thumb drive to Bob. 'Copy that email to this drive, will you? I'll need to verify that it's the source of the infection.'

Bob took the thumb drive and popped it into the front of his system. 'Do you really think we'll find anything if we monitor network traffic for this address? Surely someone will have pulled the plug by now.'

'I'm not so sure,' she replied. 'The IP address I pulled from the malware was a GES address, an inside host already flushed from Active Directory by the time we went looking for it.'

Bob's brows furrowed. 'But that requires elevated privileges. Unless someone else has control of our AD server, only someone on the inside can delete a system out of the database.'

'Exactly,' said Dana, pleased that he was following her logic. 'And, as far as this insider knows, we have no idea what the source is.'

'And until they know that, they have no incentive to throw the baby out with the bathwater,' he concluded with a smile.

'My thoughts exactly, but we'll have to move fast if we want to figure this out before Karen brings the building down around our ears.'

Mr. Porter, who'd been following their conversation in relative silence, rose to his feet. 'I don't understand everything you just said but I understand enough. You just leave Karen Forrester to me.' He exchanged a look with Bob. 'In the meantime, I want you and Ms. Sorensen working on this together. Just the two of you, nobody else, and you best be sure you don't let her out of your sight.' With that, he tipped an imaginary hat her way and strode for the door.

As soon as the door closed behind him, she turned on Bob, more than a little irritated. 'Do you believe the nerve of that man? He thinks I can't be trusted! I'm probably the only one around here he *can* trust and that's a fact.'

'He wasn't telling me to keep an eye on you, sweetheart,' replied Bob softly. 'He was telling me to keep you safe.'

CHAPTER SEVEN

The Hole

Bob was the first to speak. 'So what now?'

Dana thought about that. Knowing there was a problem and getting to the bottom of a problem were two entirely different things. They certainly knew more now than they knew before but, with an internal IP address that didn't exist and an external IP address that couldn't be traced, it remained to be seen if they knew enough.

She slid her laptop out of her bag and perched it on the edge of Bob's expansive desk. 'I threw together an ad hoc anti-virus signature yesterday. It's bare-bones but it should be sufficient to verify that the spoofed email is the source.' She connected the USB stick to her laptop and pulled up ClamAV. 'Out of curiosity,' she queried casually, 'how did you come up with the idea that we should begin our search with these financial reports as opposed to, say, anything else?'

Bob searched her face. Comprehension dawned on his. 'Oh, I get it. You think an innocent man wouldn't be able to figure it out on his own. Well, if that's the case, I have news for you. I injured my spine, not my brain.'

Dana suppressed a smile and fixed her gaze on the screen in front of her, more for herself than for him. He was pouting, and he was adorable when he pouted. If she looked at him now, she might make up her mind to forgive him and she wasn't ready to do that. Not yet, anyway.

'I'm not saying you didn't come up with the answer,' she conceded. 'I'm just saying you came up with it awful fast.'

He shrugged. 'Macros.'

He said it simply, as though it explained everything, but, from her point of view, it explained nothing. He waited for her to say something. When she didn't, he all but rolled his eyes.

'You know, little bits of code embedded in a file to increase its functionality?'

She sucked in a breath. 'I swear to God, you're worse than Mazie. I *know* what a macro is. What I don't know is why it's relevant to this discussion. Did you have a macro running in your uninjured brain when you deduced that the culprit was an email from Larry Katz?'

'Larry uses macros in all his reports,' he replied matter-of-factly. 'And since I don't read them but know that everyone else does—'

'It made it just that much easier for you to exploit them?'

'It made sense to start there,' he corrected. 'For the record, I would've infected my own system if I was the one behind all this. Better to blend in than stand out, don't you think?'

He was right, of course. It was better to blend in than stand out. Whoever was behind this attack had an intimate knowledge of Grasslands Energy Solutions, right down to the smallest detail of a routine financial report. It all pointed strongly to an insider or, at the very least, to an outsider with inside connections. It would be a mistake to start making assumptions at this point.

She looked down at her laptop screen and studied the scan results. 'Well, I'll be damned. The attachment is clean. In fact, the whole thing is clean.'

Bob sat up, his long torso straight as a board. 'How the hell can that be? Are you sure your signature is good?'

'It's good enough. If so much as a single line of that code was in here, it would find it.'

He swore and turned to his computer, rapidly clicking through screens until he found what he was looking for. 'Hand me that USB drive. I have another one for you to scan.'

She pulled the drive out of the side of her laptop and tossed it to him. He caught it easily and transferred something to it before tossing it back. The scan took only seconds.

'What did you just hand me?' she asked.

'The other email from the same day, the one that went out at 9:05 AM. Why?'

'Scan results are positive. The malicious code is embedded in the attachment.'

Bob closed his eyes and kneaded his temples. 'Damn.'

She knew what was coming but asked the question anyway. 'Where did the email originate from?'

'It originated from here,' replied Bob, finally looking up. 'Whether he knows it or not, Larry is the actual sender.'

Dana sat back, astonished. This was a first. Never in her career had she heard of anyone using bogus email to draw attention away from malicious payload attached to a legitimate message.

'That report was probably compromised before Larry ever thought about sending it,' she concluded.

'And the external IP address you pulled from the spoofed message is probably meaningless. A decoy. We're back to square one.'

He wasn't entirely wrong. The evidence was definitely taking them full circle. Was this what was happening to Detective Mercer?

'We still have the internal IP address from the malware itself,' she said resolutely. 'And we still have Bennie's notebook.'

Bob snorted. 'And how is an IP address to nowhere and a notebook full of nothing going to help us?'

'Where's your imagination? That IP address to nowhere showed up in the DHCP server logs. That means it's associated with a MAC address that might lead us to a network interface card installed in a physical system somewhere inside this building.'

'What makes you think the MAC address wouldn't be fake too?'

'Oh, come on. When was the last time you went on a good old-fashioned treasure hunt?'

He smiled half a smile and she knew she'd won him over. On the short term, at least. She happened to know he hated treasure hunts and, in this case, it would be up to him to provide most of the clues.

Bob checked the time. Against his better judgment, he'd let Dana talk him into an after-hours raid of the GES IT department. Here it was, just after 9 PM, and he was scoping out the entrance to Karen's lair as if he could actually conceal his wheelchair-ridden self from view. It didn't help that he was basically eye-level with Dana's breasts. All he had to do to get to second base was turn his head and do a face plant.

He forced himself to focus. The coast was clear. 'What are we doing here?' he whispered.

She rolled her eyes heavenward. 'I already told you,' she whispered back, 'we can't go on a treasure hunt without a map.' She pointed to the double doors leading to the IT offices. 'Everything we need is in there.'

He squared his shoulders and eased into the hallway. His key card would get them through the doors but finding the network drawings would be a different matter. And they'd need them, too. GES had a jam-packed server room and equipment stuffed into communications closets all over the building. Without a decent diagram to work from, they could be hunting this system for days.

He reminded himself that he was not, in fact, breaking and entering as he inserted his key card. He was a senior officer at this company and he had a right to be here, even if he was about to engage in petty larceny. The doors opened without event and he slid through quietly, feeling Dana at his back. The only light in the room spilled in from the security lights in the parking lot outside. There was no sound, not even the gentle hum of a copy machine. All the electronics had long since fallen into sleep mode.

Dana produced a small LED flashlight from her bag, a bag as magical as anything Mary Poppins ever carried. As far as he could tell, Dana stored everything that ever existed in the known universe inside that bag and only she had the power to remove anything from it. He'd stuck his hand in countless times before and never once latched on to the thing he was looking for.

'I think there's enough light in here to see where we're going but we'll need this for desk drawers,' she said, her voice hushed as she cast her eyes around the room. 'Where do you suppose we should start?'

He knew exactly where to start. He pointed to a poky little hallway just off the main room that led to a cramped office with no windows. 'The Hole.'

'Is that as bad as it sounds?'

He smiled in the darkness. 'It's worse than it sounds.'

And it was. Dingy, half-walled cubicles hugged the walls in a space barely large enough to meet fire codes. Every morning, four adult men piled in and they didn't leave until quitting time unless they were forced to check on a piece of equipment. Every horizontal surface in the room was a barrage of pop bottles, food wrappers, electronic components, various network cables, tools, and whatever else they could possibly cram in. The only other furniture, if you could call it that, was an oversized oscillating fan on a banged-up plastic stand and a file cabinet left over from the

1970's.

Dana risked flipping on a light to survey the strange surroundings. 'So I take it 'the hole' is short for shit hole?' She stuck her nose in the air. 'Do you smell that?'

Bob assessed the trash situation, where the contents of a folded pizza box and several fast food wrappers were laying waste to the atmosphere. Housekeeping would come through first thing in the morning but that was of no use to them. 'Let's just get what we came for,' he grumbled, wheeling himself out of her way.

Having the benefit of usable legs, Dana had the responsibility of searching the file cabinet while he looked everywhere else. She muttered enough obscenities for the both of them as she sifted through the disorganized mass of documents that probably hadn't seen the light of day in years. They searched for what seemed like hours before Dana finally found something.

'Eureka!' she hooted, brandishing an oversized drawing constructed from several pieces of copier paper taped together at the edges. She laid the network diagram on the floor and smoothed out the edges, careful to avoid touching what looked to be a combination of various food-related stains and smeared ink.

He studied the heavily soiled document and the abundance of line-outs and scrawled notes, written in more than one hand, with a grimace. Some treasure map. He reached into his pocket for his cell phone and held it out. 'Here. Use this to take a picture of what you need and let's get out of here.'

'Can't we just take it with us?'

He shook his head. 'There's enough ketchup on that thing for a double order of fries and it looks like everybody in here's had their hands on it at one time or another. I wouldn't be surprised if it wasn't the only thing in the entire cabinet they actually use.'

'But surely they won't miss it,' she protested. 'I had to dig it out from under a ream a paper. We can have it back in a day or two and they'll never know it was gone.'

'Don't mistake disorder for disorganization. If you found it in that drawer, it's because someone put it there. They're liable to notice it's missing quicker than you think.'

She seized the phone from his hand. 'There used to be a time when you enjoyed this sort of thing.'

'I never enjoyed this sort of thing.'

'You always jumped at the chance to do this stuff when we worked together.'

'How else was I supposed to get you to notice me?'

She snorted and turned her attention back to the drawing on the floor. 'You could've just asked me out, you know,' she said, snapping photos.

Bob smiled, careful to keep it to himself. If only that were true.

IP address. Check. The associated MAC address pulled from DHCP server logs. Check. The switch and switch port used by said MAC address. Check. Plan for what to do when they found the system? Vague at best. As Dana hovered outside the door to the data center and waited for Bob to punch in his access code, it occurred to her that this whole operation might come to a grinding halt in less than five minutes.

She studied his profile in the dimly lit hallway, his proud chin locked in concentration as he carefully entered the ten digit code from memory, and decided now was not the time to tell him.

Moments later, the electronic panel flashed ACCESS GRANTED and Bob swung the door wide. They were greeted by a force of cool air that swept past them into the hallway, a flow of air that worked in conjunction with thousands of tiny fans mounted inside the various rack-mounted equipment chassis to keep them from overheating. Without it, the room's temperature would skyrocket to unsafe levels in minutes. With it, however, the noise level was on par with a factory floor. Soft voices wouldn't work in here.

Bob wheeled forward, adeptly gliding around a tile marked with red tape before calling out. 'Whenever you see a tile like this,' he said, pointing to the floor, 'don't step on it. The tape means the tile's not secure; it might turn over on you if you step on it wrong.'

Dana gingerly stepped into the room, surveying the raised floor carefully as she went. The tiles were grimy, but not from dirt. The tile laminate was separating from the underlying material in several places. The grime was residue from some past attempt to glue them back down. A few tiles were marked with red tape, just as Bob said, and a few more featured gaping holes, probably left over from some past installation where an opening in the floor was needed.

'Does the network diagram tell us which rack we're looking for?' asked Bob, drawing her attention away from the hazard at her feet.

She picked a safe spot to stand and studied the images she'd captured using his phone, a task that would've been so much easier using the paper version. She flicked through the photos, zooming in on all the likely candidates, before finally finding the right one. Because it was a network diagram and not a floor plan, all she knew for certain was that the switch they were looking for was somewhere in this room. There was a number, barely legible, scrawled in green ink next to the switch name. She assumed it was a rack number but, judging by the condition of the racks and cabinets, it was anybody's guess.

She eyed the rows of racks with a frown. 'We're looking for B24. I think.'

Bob nodded and wheeled himself over to a metal table she hadn't noticed when they first walked in. It was shoved against the rear wall and, whatever it's original purpose, was presently laden with cable scraps, old backup batteries, and a variety of legacy electronic components. If she wasn't mistaken, there was fifteen years of computing history languishing on that table, which probably meant there was fifteen years worth of equipment languishing in these racks. It would be impressive if it wasn't so terrifying.

Bob snapped up a warped binder that hung off the end of the table by a tether fashioned from a length of CAT V cable. He flipped through the well-worn pages and she wondered how many times the thing went missing before they decided to tie it down. A few minutes later, he dropped the binder in disgust and wheeled back to her with a pained expression on his face.

He pointed to a row of racks to her left. 'This is section B here. According to the book, the 20's should be on the far end, near the wall.'

'Should be?'

'Do you really want to know the answer to that?'

If it was anything like the floor situation, she decided, she'd rather not know. She took her time getting to the location where the switch should be, counting as she went, aware that Bob was trailing behind. The aisle was barely wide enough for his chair and many of the cabinet doors had been left to swing open. If it was difficult for her, it was worse for him. There were a few cross-aisles that would allow them to move from one main drag to another without having to go all the way back to the center of the room but the arrangement was tight, almost claustrophobic.

She halted when they arrived at what 'should be' the 20's. As she suspected, newer equipment was sharing rack space with legacy equipment, some of which didn't even seem to be powered on. But none of that mattered. The only thing she was interested in was the 40-port switch mounted in the center of the rack nearest the wall, the twenty-fourth rack in the row.

This particular switch connected 40 individual systems to the larger network, making it possible for them to carry on conversations with each other as well as with the outside world. One of those systems was the computer she was looking for.

Realizing the neighboring rack was completely empty, she used it as a doorway to slip through to the other side where the physical ports were located. There was something plugged into every port, with some cables going up into the overhead cable tray and some going down into the space beneath the floor. Fortunately, the wire connected to the port she wanted to trace was going up.

She peered through the gaps around the equipment to make eye contact with Bob on the other side. 'I found it,' she said. 'It looks like it's going back the other way.'

'Watch your step,' he warned. 'I have to back out to a point where I can turn myself around.'

Dana followed the blue cable from the back of the switch up into the cable tray where it was bundled with several other cables. It helped that it was a particular shade of blue, slightly different from the others, giving her something to look for as she followed it along the tray until it emerged on the backside of a cabinet very near their original starting point. The cable was plugged into the network port of an ordinary server, surrounded by a dozen ordinary servers just like it.

She could see Bob making his way, a little faster now that he was finally pointed in the right direction. He joined her at the back of the server as quickly as he could manage.

'So what are we looking at?' he asked.

'Well, we're still in section B and, if that was B24, then this should be B3,' she replied, thumbing through the network diagram photos once again. She zoomed in and out, looking at the various makes, models, and serial numbers identified in each of the little boxes that represented the systems that were supposed to be in this area but found no record that would explain what this system was used for. In fact, there was no record of this system at all.

She handed the phone to Bob. 'I must be getting tired. I can't find it.'

He took the phone from her and studied the images at length. 'It's not here,' he agreed at last. 'Not in this rack, not in this section, not anywhere.'

But it was there. It was physically right there, hiding in plain sight. Was it a simple oversight or something more? There was only one way to find out.

'We need to setup a packet capture on this thing and find out what it's doing,' she said.

'I agree but how do you propose we do that?'

'Can we set up port mirroring? If we send a copy of everything going to and from this system to another port on the same switch, I can capture it using my laptop.'

Bob shook his head. 'I can't do that without going through an administrator. If this is an inside job, that'd give up our position faster than anything.'

'Can we force it?'

'Attack the switch, you mean? I doubt it. Port security is enabled.'

She closed her eyes, already regretting the words that were about to come out of her mouth. But it couldn't be helped. This wasn't her first time at the rodeo, and, although she was no stranger to installing cable taps, this was a special case that demanded special attention. It needed to be done quickly, with minimal disruption, and it needed to be well-concealed to avoid detection. In this case, she needed an expert.

'Goddammit,' she said. 'We need Max Chen.'

Dana flipped on a light at her desk, illuminating a space of about five square feet in a sea of darkness. Like most of her colleagues, she used her desk at Bellwether Data Security as a port of call, an intermediate stop between jobs. They came here, passing like ships in the night, because this was where the resources were.

Max Chen stalked up to her in the darkness, clad in jeans and a t-shirt. 'Where's Floretta?'

Dana shrugged noncommittally. 'At home in bed, I imagine.'

Max was incredulous. 'You're the one who texted me? Do you even know what time it is?'

She smiled to herself. Damn right, she knew what time it was. The fact that she drug him out of bed was the only thing that made this ordeal tolerable. 'As much as it pains me to say it, I need your help.'

Max screwed up his handsome face. 'My help? The Great and Powerful Dana Sorensen? You've got to be kidding. You really want my help? Take a number and get in line,' he spat, turning on his heel. 'And if you think I'm not filing a formal complaint over this, you got another thing comin'.'

'You're not going to file a complaint,' she taunted. 'I was on the committee that hired you, remember? I trained you, I mentored you, and, as I recall, it was my work you took credit for on your desperate climb up the corporate ladder. Some people might say I made you. So, yes, I'm asking for a favor in the middle of the goddamn night. I gave you a career and now I want something back.'

Max halted and spun around. 'I had a right to claim credit for that work.'

'You exaggerated your contributions and you know it,' she shot back. 'And for what? A pat on the head and a few juicy bones?'

'You don't know what you're talking about.'

She slid the offer letter out of her bag and handed it to him. 'I know more than you think.'

She watched the vein at his temple jump as he devoured every word. 'Is this a joke?'

'Am I laughing?'

'It's not signed,' he said, handing the letter back.

'No, it's not,' she agreed. 'You know, I used to want this more than anything.' She laughed at her own naivete, a laugh laced with contempt for the both of them. 'But then you probably understand that more than anyone here.'

He did understand. She could see it in his face. 'Are you saying you don't want it anymore?' he asked. There was hope in his voice.

'I'm saying I'm undecided.' She watched as his face fell and silently kicked herself for her meanness. The game had gone on long enough. 'But I could be persuaded.'

Max's head shot up. He began to understand the terms of the bargain. 'What do you need me to do?'

Dana and Bob exchanged looks as Max inspected the GES server room. He was less than impressed. 'Please tell me you're not serious.' He looked at Bob. 'You left BDS for *this*?'

'We're serious,' quipped Dana, waving Bob off, determined that nothing should happen to Max until he'd served his purpose. 'And don't step on the tiles marked in red tape.'

'Why not?'

'Because you're liable to fall through and break your precious little neck,' snapped Bob.

Max looked at the floor as though he were walking on the back of some great serpent and pulled his backpack closer. Dana could feel him inches from her back as she led the way to the server. He stepped where she stepped, his hand at the ready in case he needed to use her body to support his, as if she could. She didn't hold it against him, though. Max wouldn't be Max if he wasn't looking out for number one.

'This is it,' she said, pointing to the back of the server they'd found only a couple of hours earlier.

Max set his backpack on the floor and began inspecting the server and surrounding rack space. 'So what's the deal with this system?'

'We don't know,' said Bob.

Max quirked an eyebrow. 'You don't know? Is it rogue?'

'We don't know that, either,' said Dana. 'We think it may be linked to a malware attack.'

'Is the attack ongoing?'

'For now. The IT director is trying to shut it down, though, so we need to act fast.'

Max nodded. She knew he understood the situation perfectly.

The attacker almost always had the upper hand in these cases. Tempting as it was to pull the plug, they would learn more if they kept their distance.

He pulled a slender, compact network tap out of his backpack and handed it to her while he fished around for his cable tools. 'Have you imaged the drive yet?'

Dana shook her head. 'I don't want to take the system offline any longer than we have to until we know more.'

Max nodded again. 'Well this part should be relatively painless. The LAN cables are a mess but that should work to our advantage. Someone already did us a favor and chunked out a nice opening in this tile here and, as you can see, some of the cables already go that direction. If there's a spare power outlet under the floor, I can attach the tap and the collection device to the underside of the panel. In fact, if we can find some spare cable in this same color, the whole setup should be completely invisible. The hardest thing will be making sure we don't disturb the dust.'

Bob piped up. 'How much data will we be able to capture at a time?'

Max pulled a sleek tablet PC out of his bag along with an external solid state drive. 'This drive will hold about 250 Gig but you can always swap it out for a bigger one if you need to.'

'Why didn't you just bring a regular hard drive?' asked Bob, somewhat irritated. 'It'd hold twice the data for half the price.'

Max smiled. 'Would you believe I thought noise would be a factor?'

Bob grimaced at the jab. Dana couldn't help but smile. Solid state drives were silent. The hard drive in the tablet PC would be the same. No revving, no whirring. Paired with a completely passive network tap, a person could put their ear to the floor in a quiet room and not hear a thing.

Max worked quickly. Bob fetched a tile lifter from the vicinity of the metal table. Dana made note of where it had been as Max slapped the suction cups down onto the flat surface and squeezed. The tile lifted effortlessly and Max slid in up to his waist as though he were slipping into a shallow swimming pool. He shined a flashlight under the floor until he found an available outlet.

'It's a longer stretch than I'd like but we can do it,' he assured them. 'Let's just hope it's live.' He eased down to his knees and shimmied into position. After a brief bout of violent cussing, Max resurfaced and tested his work. 'We have power,' he announced triumphantly.

Using brackets he fashioned himself from metal flashing and a series of short screws, Max mounted the network tap and collection device securely to the bottom of the tile. With that in place, he relocated the LAN cable from the back of the server and replaced it with a patch cable made from a length of matching scrap Bob found lodged under a cabinet on the other side of the room. The circuit was complete. Information now flowed from the switch, through the network tap, to the server and back the other way. From this point on, they would know every move the server made on the network.

Satisfied with the software settings, Max lifted himself out of the floor and eased the tile back into place. He tossed his tools into his backpack while Dana returned the tile lifter to where Bob found it. As a final touch, Max artfully arranged the cables so that everything appeared as it should, careful to avoid disturbing the dust and debris already present. Dana was impressed. The installation was flawless. The server couldn't have lost its network connection for more than 30 seconds. More importantly, if anybody bothered to investigate, they would find nothing out of place.

Max wasted no time. 'Do we still have a deal?'

'We have a deal.'

Bob, unaware of their bargain, was confused. 'What deal?'

Before Dana could say anything, however, Bob's hand flew up to silence her. There was a sound, barely perceptible, just outside the door. It had pitch. Someone was entering an access code into the key pad. There was no time to coordinate their response; instead, they each scrambled to find whatever hiding spot they could among the racks. Bob, at least, had the wherewithal to hit the light switch as he rolled past. Where he rolled to, in complete darkness, she had no idea.

Her heart was pounding so loud she could barely hear the door when it opened. She hugged the nearest cabinet to hold herself steady, hoping against hope that her position wouldn't be compromised the second the lights came back up. Everything in here was designed with ventilation in mind. There were openings, both large and small, everywhere.

The lights flashed to life as someone, a man, ambled in holding a laptop. Fortunately, he took no notice of her. She frantically searched the room for Bob and Max but there was no sign of either of them, thank God. Her view was largely obstructed by racks and equipment but she could make out a few details through the gaps. It was definitely a man. Tallish, red hair, receding hair line, lots of freckles. Beyond that, all she could make out was a worn-out t-shirt that said I Heart Pr0n and a pair of blue jeans. And, dammit, he was standing—no, *crouching*—on the exact tile that concealed Max's network tap.

He was focused on the laptop in his hands. There was a hint of a furrowed brow as he worked but no indication that he discovered the tap. She didn't dare check the time on her phone but she knew it had to be going on 1 AM. For all she knew, this guy was just a system administrator here to do scheduled maintenance. It was common enough, even at this late hour.

After what seemed like ages, she heard the laptop snap shut. Without so much as a glance in her direction, the man shuffled out just as he came in, flipping off the light as he went. He was gone but no one moved a muscle.

Max was the first to speak. 'Who the hell was that?' he called into the darkness.

Bob replied from somewhere on the opposite side of the room. 'That,' he said, 'was Carl. And that's a problem.'

The light snapped back on. Max had found the switch. Bob, bless his heart, was sprawled out on the floor, apparently forced to abandon his chair in the chaos. He pushed himself up using his powerful arms and drug his chair towards him. Locking the wheels into place, he rotated his body and hoisted himself up effortlessly.

Or at least it appeared effortless. She could make out the taut lines of his muscled arms and chest through the fabric of his shirt. He'd always been a powerfully built man but he was even more so now. She wasn't the only one who noticed. Max looked at Bob warily, suddenly aware that a man didn't need to have working legs to be strong. Or dangerous.

'Why is that a problem?' she asked, dragging her eyes away from Bob's physique.

'It's a problem because he doesn't work here. I fired him six months ago.'

CHAPTER EIGHT

The North Door

Unlike Floretta, Jeremy Stiles looked out of place in the sleek offices of Bellwether Data Security. An ordinary man in every sense of the word, Dana was convinced he would disappear into the walls of a more traditional environment like one of those men everyone sees but can never remember. Here, however, he stuck out like a sore thumb, a fact his ordinary nature seemed to resent. She couldn't help but wonder if this ordinary man wouldn't also be a nice man if he worked anywhere else.

'You respectfully decline?' sputtered Jeremy for the third time in a row. His cheeks flamed. 'Floretta damn near wore me out talking about you, insisted I'd be a damn fool if I didn't hire you, and here you are, telling me you don't want the job I didn't even want to hire you for in the place. You got some nerve, you know that?' He sucked in a breath. 'Do you know what I had to go through to make the offer without a hiring committee? But you don't care about that do you? No, sir. I'll have you know there are thousands of people, maybe even tens of thousands of people, who would leave everything they have and everyone they know for an opportunity like this in today's economy!'

Dana was impressed by the uncharacteristic outburst but she wasn't fooled by it. If Jeremy was smarting over anything it was that he'd let himself be bullied by Floretta for no good reason. And if he wanted to have a conniption fit over that, well, he'd just have to get in line like everybody else.

'I'm sure you're right,' she said simply, rising from her seat. She moved toward the door. She said what she came to say, it was time to leave. 'Thank you for your time and be sure to congratulate Max for me once he accepts the job.' For however long it lasted. If she knew Max, he'd have Jeremy's job within two years.

'Max isn't available. Or at least he won't be for long.'

She stopped short. 'I beg your pardon?'

Jeremy hesitated, apparently realizing he'd said too much. 'Look,' he said finally, his voice low. 'You didn't hear this from me but Floretta announced her retirement a couple weeks back, if you want to call it that. Now don't ask me when she's leaving, exactly, because I don't know but it's coming up soon. The way things are shaping up, Max will be taking her place.'

She was stunned beyond words. An ugly premonition formed in her mind. 'Does he know?'

'Officially? I doubt it.'

'What about unofficially?'

'I'd be shocked if he didn't know something was coming. He's been gunning for that job at least a year, probably longer.'

Dana closed her eyes and struggled to process the information overwhelming her mind. Were Max and Floretta co-conspirators or enemies? If she was honest, it didn't really matter. She knew them both too well to be truly surprised one way or the other.

Her eyes stung but she didn't cry; instead, she gathered her bag closer and left Jeremy with as much grace as she could manage. Then she strode to the elevators and punched the button for the ground floor where human resources was located. There was something she needed to do and she'd better do it now before she chickened out.

Bob studied the two rows of computer monitors, mounted one on top of the other, across a long counter spanning four workstations whose boundaries were lost amid the clutter long ago. The gray laminate surface was barely visible beneath a sea of multi-line telephones, well-worn binders embellished with sticky notes, capless ink pens, flashlights of all sizes, keys and key cards, and an assortment of coffee cups with the coffee rings to match. Floating above this mess were the monitors, each displaying the output of anywhere from six to nine cameras that were positioned throughout GES. He came in here to find out how an employee who'd been terminated months ago could just waltz into the building, sight unseen, but now he wondered how it was that it didn't happen more often.

He could see Andy Paulson, one of the younger security guards, rummaging around in the storage closet at the back of the room. Unfortunately, Andy did not see him. Emerging from the closet with an armload of printer paper, Andy's lanky frame buckled over Bob, who took a ream of paper straight in the forehead before it slammed into his crotch.

Andy unfurled himself with the elegance of a newborn gazelle. 'Oh my God. Oh my God. I'm so sorry Mr. Leroy. Are you okay?'

Bob thrust the ream of paper into Andy's clumsy hands, simultaneously pushing him away, as he used his free hand to protect his manhood from further damage. It registered somewhere in his brain that the sandy-haired behemoth had asked him a question but the rest of him was too busy deciding whether he should faint or vomit to answer. Andy, for his part, froze to the spot where Bob pushed him, apparently afraid to breathe.

'Don't stand there like an idiot,' growled Bob through clenched teeth. 'Pick up all this goddamned paper!'

'Yes, sir. Oh God, sir, are you sure you're all right?' He gestured to Bob's groin tentatively. 'Did I hurt you? I mean, can you actually, um, feel, uh, anything? You know, down there?'

Bob stared up at the boy, wholly exasperated. Thirty-three vertebrae in the human spine, thirty-one pairs of spinal nerves, and yet, somehow, he was destined to spend the rest of his natural life answering just one question. 'Yes, I have sensation *down there*. Down there works perfectly fine, thank you. Or at least it did before you dropped a five-pound weight on it,' he spat.

He watched as Andy nervously collected the reams of paper off the floor and stacked them under the counter near a large laser printer.

'Why wasn't the door to this room locked?' he demanded.

Andy looked up. 'Wasn't it?'

'If it was locked, then how do you explain me?'

'Oh, right. Well, it's supposed to be locked.'

Bob swore inwardly. The list of transgressions was never ending, it seemed. 'There was an employee that used to work here, a man named Carl Payne. Do you recognize the name?'

Andy nodded. 'I remember Carl. Red hair, older guy, maybe in his late forties? He used to work in IT, didn't he?'

'That's the one,' said Bob, not entirely sure he agreed that 'late forties' qualified as 'older.' 'He was terminated from this company six months ago. I fired him myself. I'm sure you can imagine, then, how surprised I was when he showed up inside our data center at one o'clock this morning.'

Andy's eyes went wide. 'How'd he get in? I was here when the night guards came off shift. They said nobody came through the main entrance.'

'The north door is equipped with an electronic cipher lock. Would he still have the code?'

Andy shook his head. 'He's not supposed to. We change it every month, sometimes more than that.'

Bob raked his hand through his hair and glanced up at the monitors. 'Is there a camera on that door?'

'There's a camera on all the outside doors.'

'Is the footage recorded?'

'Yes.'

A dull, repetitive thump was sounding in Bob's head. He focused on his breathing and reached for the emergency migraine pill he kept in the inside pocket of his jacket. He swallowed it without water and hoped to God it would kick in before he did something to this kid that he'd later regret.

'Will you please pull it up so I can see it?'

Finally understanding what was being asked of him, Andy folded himself into one of the chairs pushed against the long counter and accessed the video archive for the north door. As expected, Carl sauntered up just before 12:30 AM and punched in the code. The door swung open and he disappeared inside the building. At 1:10 AM, he left the same way he came in.

Bob swore. 'Save that to disc,' he instructed. It figured that a character like Carl would have no trouble getting his hands on the code to the cipher lock. It was possible he had a buddy on the inside who was willing to give it to him but it was more likely that he was looking over someone's shoulder as they came into the building. It would be easy enough. To anyone outside of IT, Carl would seem like any other random employee.

There was another code, however, that he couldn't get so easily.

'Can you get to the logs for the access panel outside the data center?'

'Sure.'

Bob sighed. What was it his mama used to say? Bless his little pea pickin' heart? That was Andy to a T.

Bob spoke slowly. 'Can you pull it up for me? I want to know if Carl is still using his old code to get into the server room.'

'Oh, right.'

Andy clicked through a maze of screens, finally landing on a list of everyone who entered the data center over the last thirty days. The record for last night clearly showed Bob entering the facility twice, first with Dana and then again later with Max in tow. And then came Carl, although, according to this, it wasn't Carl.

'Well, I'll be damned,' he muttered, mostly to himself. 'Who gave Ruby Hornbuckle an access code to the server room? She's not even a system administrator.'

Andy shrugged. 'We don't have information like that in here. We don't give out those codes anymore, not since Miss Forrester came on board.'

'If you don't give them out, who does?'

'That's what I'm saying. Miss Forrester gives them out. Or maybe she has one of her people do it. It was one of the changes she made when she got here. If you want to know more, ask Bill.'

Bob groaned inwardly. Bill had worked in the building since 1968, well before GES came along. He was a doddering old man if ever there was one, easy pickings for someone like Karen. She probably had him convinced she was in charge of the whole company.

He looked back at the screen. 'Can you show me the history of just one person?'

'Sure can.'

'Then let's see Ruby's activity for the past twelve months.'

Andy complied. The report was blistering. Apparently, 'Ruby Hornbuckle,' had been entering the data center once every two weeks or so for months, always after hours.

The seriousness of the situation was apparently not lost on Andy. 'This is bad, ain't it?'

Bob decided to give him a break. 'Yes, Andy, this is bad.'

'What do you want us to do?'

'Install a camera outside the server room. Anybody goes in that room, I want to know. And keep tabs on our friend Carl. Don't approach him until I give the go-ahead, but don't lose track of him, either. Do you understand?'

Andy nodded.

'As of right now, everything to do with that room is confidential. You report to me and no one else.'

Dana plopped a brown paper bag in Bob's lap.

He winced. 'What's this?'

'Chicken salad on rye for you, turkey and bacon for me, a couple bottles of water, and two pudding cups,' she said, matter-of-factly. 'In case you didn't notice, I'm not one to miss meals. Why are you flinching? Are you hurt?'

'Let's just say you're not the first person to drop something in my lap today.' He eased the bag open to peer inside. 'Only two pudding cups? Did you remember the spoons?'

She smiled. 'Both puddings are for you. The spoon is at the bottom. Although I don't know why you need one, you're just going to inhale them anyway.'

She glanced at the time on her phone as she trailed behind him en route to the data center. It was just now 8 PM, less than 24 hours since the network tap was installed. They were bound to have captured thousands of packets of data by now, she just hoped they also snagged a few they could use.

She looked around while Bob punched in his code. Something caught her eye. 'Was that camera here yesterday?' she asked, pointing to the ceiling.

Bob shook his head as he pushed the door open. 'No. I had it installed today. Do you think it's too obvious?'

'Not at all,' she replied as she followed him in, letting the door click shut behind her. 'I doubt I would've noticed it at all if I didn't happen to look that way.'

'Well, let's just hope Carl doesn't also happen to look that way the next time he shows up.'

'Next time? You're going to let him back in?'

'I want the bastard on tape.'

Bob filled her in on Carl's activities while they ate their sandwiches. She sat cross-legged on the floor, using the flattened paper bag as a seat to protect her clothes from the grubby floor. From her vantage point, Bob was as tall as ever and sexy as hell with his five o'clock shadow and shirt-sleeves rolled up to his muscled forearms. She'd almost forgotten how masculine he was.

When he finished his story, she twisted the cap off a bottle of water and took a long draw. It was a lot of information to take in but there did seem to be a common denominator.

'Why Ruby?'

Bob looked confused. 'Why not Ruby? When you think about it, she's the perfect cover. Her name pops up and no one thinks a thing about it whether they should or not.'

'I think there's more to it than that, I just can't figure out what,' she said with a sigh. Somehow, Ruby was a part of this and she knew she wouldn't sleep until she figured it out. Her mind would keep going back to it, pushing at it from every angle like a loose tooth.

Bob wadded up his sandwich wrapper and stuffed it into the nested plastic cups that once held a generous serving of chocolate pudding. 'Are you ready to see what we got?'

Dana hauled herself to her feet, brushed off the crumbs, and salvaged the paper bag from the floor to put their trash in. She'd have to hold on to it. All things considered, it was probably a bad idea to leave evidence of their shared meal in the overflowing trash bin by the door.

'As ready as I can be.'

Bob fetched the tile lifter from where it was tossed the night before and held the tile aloft while she retrieved the external storage device. She was still pissed at Max but she had to hand it to him, everything seemed to be working exactly as intended.

She slipped her laptop out of her bag and connected the drive while Bob put the tile back down and situated himself next to her. The amount of data was surprising. It was more than she dared hoped for. She passed the laptop up to Bob and rummaged through her bag for her notes.

'I don't know about you,' she said, flipping to a page with a list of IP addresses, 'but I really don't want to be in here all night. Let's start with these and see what we get.'

Bob didn't argue as he carefully typed in the IP addresses she called out. A few moments later, he gave a low whistle. 'Well, I'll be damned. Wait till you get a load of this.'

He passed the laptop back to her and looked on as she scrolled through the results. Jackpot. She'd called off the IP address of every system known to be infected with the creptio spyware and, without exception, here was the proof connecting those systems to this server.

'It's a good thing Karen's people don't know what to do with a perfectly good network signature,' she mused. 'We might have missed out on this altogether.'

The attacker, it seemed, was leveraging the server in two ways. First, as a central repository for the text files being generated by the keylogger and, second, as a means to access each of the infected systems through their respective backdoors. It was all very neat and tidy, in its own way, but it didn't explain why Carl was making routine visits to the data center. He was obviously remoting in on a regular basis, the timestamps proved that much. And if he controlled the server like she thought he did, there was nothing he could do on-site that he couldn't also do from home.

Bob looked at her. 'You're wondering why Carl keeps coming back here, why he risks being seen. I'm wondering the same thing.' He paused, thinking. 'How is he accessing the server when he's not here?'

It was a fair question. After much digging, Dana grimaced. 'He set up an SSH tunnel. He established a secure connection to the server from a remote system. The traffic is encrypted.' She squinted at the screen. 'And that's not all.'

'What's not all?'

'I see where an unknown remote system establishes a secure connection with the local server, followed by traffic from that server to the infected systems. The only good news there is that everything on the GES side was shuttled around in plaintext. Let's call that *Event A.* '

'Event A? So I take it there's an Event B?'

She nodded. 'That would be a second SSH connection established by a computer inside the network several hours later.'

'Inside the network? You mean inside the GES network?'

'Yup. And considering a *third* SSH connection was established almost immediately after that, this time from the server to a remote host, I'd say your insider was using the server as an intermediary.'

'You're saying someone inside the company set up an SSH tunnel with the server and then used the server to set up another SSH tunnel with a system outside the company.'

'That's exactly what I'm saying. And judging by the volume of packets, I'd be willing to bet they were sending huge amounts of data to that system, too.'

Bob swore. 'Is this what Carl was doing while he was here last night? Exfiltrating data from our network?'

Dana shook her head. 'The timestamps don't match. In fact, there's no evidence that Carl did anything on the network while he was here. Whatever he did, he must've done it on the system itself.'

'Why would he come here to do something like that?'

'I don't know. Maybe he just likes knowing he can—some

people are like that.'

Bob swore violently. 'We have to be missing something. Maybe he has a customer. Could he be gathering the information one way, packaging it somehow, and then sending it directly to the buyer another way?'

'That's as likely a scenario as any. If he can get into the server room, there's no reason he can't get somewhere else inside the company. He might also have someone on the inside helping him. It's worth pointing out, though, that a lot more data went out than was collected in the same time period and the IP addresses of both remote hosts are different.'

Bob massaged his temples. 'Okay,' he said, gathering his thoughts, 'we have to assume the ISP won't tell us who belongs to either of those IP addresses without a court order and the encrypted data is as good as gone. That leaves us with the plaintext. How quickly can you isolate those files?'

She was already one step ahead of him. She ran the packet capture file through a software tool specifically designed to extract and reconstruct files based on their unique file signatures and reviewed the output. The results were impressive. Someone was sure having a field day with GES management. There were at least two dozen different documents here.

She opened a text file first. 'Who is wileyj?'

'John Wiley is the head of research and development. Why?'

Dana scanned the document, trying to avoid absorbing too many details. It was impossible to deny that her field of expertise involved a certain degree of voyeurism. Everything in front of her may have already happened but the fact didn't make her any less a witness. John Wiley thought he was alone when he entered his username and password into a proprietary GES web app. He assumed his email messages were private. He never suspected a thing was out of place when he made his revisions to a highly sensitive report and then used his personal credit card to buy flowers for his wife online. And, yet, here it was, displayed for all the world to see.

She looked at Bob. She didn't need to say much. 'He's been compromised.'

Bob swore. 'I think it's safe to say they've all been compromised. What else did you find?'

She scanned through the list of files and opened them in succession. 'Aside from the keystrokes, there are documents that seem to be related to GES environmental policies and a handful of invoices.'

'Invoices?'

'Chemicals. Hydrochloric acid, acetaldehyde, ethylene glycol, polyacrylamide, and a bunch of other things I can't pronounce.' She looked up. 'Why would someone be interested in invoices for chemicals?'

Bob raked a hand through his hair. 'Because the chemicals are used in hydraulic fracturing.'

'Okay, I can appreciate why a competitor might be interested in a proprietary formula for fracking fluid, assuming they could even piece it together from a handful of invoices, but what can they learn from the company's environmental practices?'

'Nothing. Whoever went after this information isn't a competitor.'

His meaning was clear. 'You think he means to hand it over to a watchdog group?' It was a startling thought. She wasn't bothered by it in principle—in her personal opinion, fracking was a questionable practice under the best of circumstances—but the man she saw sneaking in last night didn't strike her as a dedicated environmentalist. There had to be more to it than that.

Bob was too distracted to comment, probably busy figuring out how to break the news to his superiors. She flipped the lid closed on her laptop and studied the server. It was completely unremarkable, surrounded by dozens of machines just like it. It was also completely covered in a layer of dust. A problem, for sure, but not insurmountable.

She looked at Bob. 'Enough with the pity party. We need answers, so let's just open the damn thing and be done with it.'

'You can't be serious,' Bob objected. 'You shut that thing off and the whole world will know what we're up to. Besides,' he added, eyeballing the server skeptically, 'there's no way to get the case open without leaving marks. Carl will see.'

'There's always a way,' Dana insisted. 'And he already knows something's up. It's just a matter of time. We need the contents of that hard drive and you know it.'

Bob was unconvinced. 'Okay, Miss Smartypants, how exactly do you propose we do this?'

She studied his face. Clearly, he'd forgotten who he was

dealing with. 'I have a set of tools and a forensic duplicator in the trunk of my car courtesy of BDS. As for leaving marks, we'll just have to be careful.'

'And what happens when he realizes the thing is offline?'

'Does it matter?'

'It absolutely does matter. I want the bastard.'

She wracked her brain for a solution. She didn't like the idea of taking a live image. Even if they could login to the server, and they probably couldn't, it was almost certainly being monitored. Pulling the LAN cable was pointless. If they were going to do that, they might as well shut it down.

It was a risk either way and, frankly, the odds were better going the traditional route. And despite the fact that Carl was caught on the premises, they would still need every bit of evidence they could get their hands on if they had any hope of convincing a jury. She couldn't keep the attacker from compromising the original drive between now and then but she could certainly know what she was looking for when the time came, and sometimes that was half the battle.

An idea formed in her mind. 'If we take several of these systems offline at the same time,' she asked, 'how quickly would your people respond?'

Bob blinked. 'Depends on what's offline. As long as network connectivity isn't affected, they probably won't know anything's wrong until they start getting calls at the help desk.' His eyes narrowed, 'Why, what are you thinking?'

'I'm thinking we could stage an outage,' she replied, running her eyes across an ancient uninterruptible power supply that was clearly overdue for servicing. Nearly every UPS in the room was in the same condition. 'If we take a handful of non-critical servers offline that are all connected to the same UPS and leave them that way, then what would keep the sys admins from assuming it was a power problem?'

'They could check to see if there was a surge, they could test the UPS, they could do any number of things,' Bob reminded her.

'Yes, but will they bother?' she challenged. 'My guess is they'll just come in here, reboot everything, and then it'll be back to business as usual.' She knew she was right. Given the state of things, the UPS would probably have to fail completely before anyone lifted a finger. Or opened a checkbook.

'And what if Carl doesn't try to find out what happened? The plan only works if he believes it too.'

'He'll find out. Besides, I don't think he'll have to do a thing. I think he has an inside contact who will look into it for him. How else could he be so confident that he won't get caught coming in here at night?' She looked at Bob expectantly, waiting for him to decide. He didn't hesitate long.

'Fine,' he said. 'We'll do it your way. How long will it take?'

Not as long as it would've taken using a write blocker back at the lab, as it turned out. Getting the server out of the rack was the most difficult part. The server was dirty and it had to stay dirty to avoid suspicion and that meant neither of them could get a good grip on the thing. They narrowly avoided catastrophe twice. Fortunately, she'd snagged the newest, fastest portable forensic duplicator in her company's arsenal. Max had already submitted a request for it, of course, but the people responsible for issuing the equipment liked her better.

The high-speed duplicator transferred data at rates of gigabytes per minute, making short work of the modestly sized server hard drive. It was also helpful that the equipment was designed to make two evidence drives simultaneously. If she couldn't keep the original drive in her custody, at least she could have a pristine copy to hold back in reserve. When it was done, both evidence drives went into anti-static bags, the original drive went back into the server, and the server, rather carefully, went back to its original location.

She gathered her tools and equipment, careful to avoid disturbing the environment any more than they already had, while Bob used the network diagram photos on his phone to pick out servers to take offline. By the looks of it, he was none too sure about his choices.

He smiled his odd little smile. 'Well, either I turned off a bunch of unimportant things or I turned off every important thing we have. I don't think we should stick around to find out.'

Dana agreed whole-heartedly. As they made their way out of the data center and down the hall, her body screamed for bed. She squashed the feeling. She wanted to know what the server hard drive had to say about this whole business and she wasn't leaving until she had her answer.

She was just about to ask if they should use her office or his when his phone issued a happy little tri-toned jingle.

'It's a text message,' he informed her as he slid the phone out of his pocket. He faced darkened slightly. He spoke in a low voice and began pushing her toward the stairwell. 'It's from one of the night guards. Carl just entered the building through the north door.'

Dana looked around the hallway frantically. 'Where is the north door?' she whispered.

He put his fingers to his lips as he opened the stairwell door and pushed her through, following close behind in his chair. Within seconds, she could hear footfalls, barely discernible through the door, heading their way. When it sounded like he'd passed, Dana risked a peek through the small glass pane above the door handle. She saw the back of Carl's head, with his unmistakable, scraggly red hair, as he rounded the corner down the hallway where they'd just been a few minutes ago.

She hauled in a breath and leaned against the wall, hugging her bag to her body. Bob was holding the forensic duplicator, safely stowed in its black case, in his lap. They were well out of sight of the little window. She half-expected Carl to spot the surveillance camera and come running back in their direction but, instead, there was the distant sound of an access code being entered followed by a soft thud. He was in.

Bob sat across from her, staring at her in silence. But he wasn't staring at her. Or at least he wasn't staring at her face. She glanced down and realized her shirt was gaping at the neck, open all the way down to the top of her bra. It must have come undone in all the commotion. She noticed a small cut just above her cleavage, very shallow. When she touched it, a small amount of blood came off on her hand. She rubbed it between her fingers, wondering what could have caused it. Her hand suddenly flew to her neck.

Bob rolled forward with a start, no longer bothering to remain hidden from view. His face was etched with concern as he reached up to inspect her injury himself. 'What happened?' he demanded hoarsely. 'Are you okay? Tell me you're okay.'

'I'm okay. But the ring,' she gasped, 'the ring is gone.'

CHAPTER NINE

Greed, Plain and Simple

Bob stared up at Dana's gaping shirt and the small cut on her chest. A thin line of blood, already beginning to dry, trailed along the ample curve of her breast until it finally disappeared into a soft valley concealed by a lace-edged bra. He struggled to understand what any of it had to do with a ring.

He pulled a cotton handkerchief from his pocket and pressed it on her wound. She winced. 'This is mostly clean,' he promised. 'When I'm not rushing to the aid of women, I use it to clean my glasses. What do you mean the ring is gone? What ring?'

She blushed. In the shadows of the dimly lit stairwell, it struck him as a rather becoming shade of pink.

She was hesitant. 'Your grandmother's ring.'

He was too stunned to speak. He'd proposed to her with that ring five years ago. His grandmother had given it to him when he was still a boy. She thought the sapphire matched the blue of his eyes, his genetic inheritance from a grandfather he never met. 'Hold on to that,' she'd said, 'and, when you're all growed up, you give it to the girl you're gonna marry.' He remembered the weight of it in his hand all those years ago. He was so awestruck by the sparkling blue gem, surrounded by a ring of tiny diamonds and set on a gold band, that he forgot to tell his grandmother he was too smart to ever get married.

And then he met Dana and realized he'd be a fool not to. He gave her the ring on a spring afternoon and never asked for it back. His mind was made up, even as their relationship disintegrated. Either he married Dana or he didn't marry at all, and that meant the ring belonged to her. Now she was telling him she lost it as if losing it was the most important part of the story.

An image flashed in his mind. The gold chain she wore, the thing under her shirt she kept fiddling with. 'You've been wearing it around your neck all this time?'

She said nothing but managed a nod. The movement was barely perceptible but it was enough. He drug her away from the wall into his lap until they were face to face and then he did the thing he should've had the courage to do days ago. He kissed the daylights out of her. Much to his surprise, she kissed him right back.

Gasping for air, she finally broke the kiss and rested her forehead against his. There was a special satisfaction in how she clutched his shoulders. He liked knowing that he'd rendered her speechless, that her heart raced because he made it race. If she still carried his ring, it could only mean that somewhere, deep down, she still belonged to him.

When she did speak, she was breathless. 'I'm sorry.'

'For what? For the kiss?'

She shook her head. 'For the ring. I think it must have gotten caught on something in the server room.'

He eyed the cut on her chest. 'Didn't you feel it?'

'I remember feeling a little tug, maybe even a pinch, but we were sliding the server back into place and I didn't dare take my eyes off it.' She let out a frustrated sigh. 'I can't believe we went through all that trouble just for me to blow it like this.'

He gently tugged the fabric of her shirt together and began buttoning the small buttons. One of them was missing. 'You didn't blow anything, sweetheart. If the ring fell off in the rack, you can bet it landed where even we won't find it easily.'

She indulged him with a smile and straightened herself up. He slid his phone out of his pocket and called the security guard station. Under the circumstances, he was grateful there were no cameras in this part of the stairwell.

He was still speaking with the security guard when he heard a heavy door close. The guard confirmed that Carl just left the data center. Bob waited for his shadow to pass before saying anything else.

'Is he leaving out the north door again?'

'Yes, sir. Do you want us to intercept him?'

'No, but I do want you to change the cipher lock combination the second he clears the parking lot. And keep changing it. I don't want that bastard coming and going as he pleases anymore, understood?'

The security guard did understand. He slipped his phone back into his pocket and motioned for Dana to follow him. A quick check of the hallway confirmed the coast was clear of everything, including the ring.

The data center was completely unchanged. He didn't honestly expect to see anything different but it unnerved him to think what Carl might have been doing in here. If they installed a network tap and imaged a hard drive without disturbing so much as a speck of dust, there was no telling what a character like Carl could get away with.

'It's not here,' Dana gasped from where she crouched on the floor. He could hear the panic in her voice. 'It's not here.'

He grabbed the tile lifter. The ring had to be there somewhere. Carl would've had to walk right over it to find it, and what were the odds of that when they didn't walk over it on their way out?

'Do you still have that flashlight in your bag?'

She did. Their examination of the area was thorough but yielded nothing except a single button that he found resting in the dust at the base of the rack. He held it up to her shirt to confirm it was a match and then handed it to her.

She looked at it with disgust before stuffing it in her pocket, where it likely faced a violent end in the gentle cycle. She was more frantic than he'd ever seen her. 'He found it,' she declared, threatening to pace a hole into the floor, completely unconcerned about her proximity to the tiles marked with red tape. 'He had to have. That son of a bitch found it and he took it.' She stopped to looked at Bob, consternation evident in her face. 'What do we do now?'

He scanned the room, picking out the servers that he'd taken offline just before Carl's arrival. They were still offline. All, that is, except the one server Carl cared about.

'We had this server offline for, what, an hour before he came charging through that door?'

Dana nodded. 'Just over an hour I think. Why?'

'There must be something pretty damn important on this server if he's willing to bust in here at the first sign of trouble. We need to look at that hard drive.'

'What about the ring?'

'Let him keep the ring for now. He'll find out who it belongs to soon enough.'

Dana tapped the keyboard of her laptop with unsteady hands. Despite her best efforts, her body thrummed with an awareness that simply did not share her interest in the screen in front of her. If Bob's restlessness was anything to go by, he was having the same problem. She reached for the bottle of water Bob had produced from the mini fridge in his assistant's office. It was a cheap substitute for a cold shower but the alternative was too complicated to consider. For the moment, anyway.

Carl's server turned out to be a Linux box with no apparent purpose beyond gathering intel from infected systems. In all likelihood, the server was on a list somewhere to be decommissioned or, worse, on a list of things already decommissioned. Out of sight, out of mind, lost in a sea of sameness.

'Do you see anything?' asked Bob, interrupting her thoughts.

'Files, lots of files, mostly stored in a hidden partition,' she replied absently as she sifted through the filenames.

It was all more of the same. Text files containing the keystrokes of infected users, documents describing GES environmental policies and practices—all constructed from industry standard boilerplate—more invoices, a handful of press releases, and even a few publicly releasable government reports. There was also a directory buried in the mix, imaginatively named 'creptio'. She expected the directory to contain application files for the spyware; instead, she found documents, or, rather, image files of scanned documents.

She nudged Bob. 'Look at this. I think it's a contract of some kind. There's a ton of them in this folder.'

Bob, who'd been squinting at the screen, gave up and dug his reading glasses out of his desk drawer. 'It's a lease,' he explained after a brief examination. 'More specifically, it's an oil and gas lease.' He pointed to a spot on the screen. 'It shows Grasslands Energy Solutions as the lessee here and the lessor happens to be a private landowner named Hart McConnell. It looks like a standard contract but it expired some eight years ago.' He shook his head. 'Unless there's a current lease on file, I can't imagine what Carl thinks he can do with this.'

Dana clicked open a few more documents until she realized her error. Carl used a naming convention. The files were meant to be organized by name, not by type or date. In this case, he used names in the literal sense. Each cluster of files was identified by the surname of individual lessors, landowners who either currently leased their mineral rights to GES or who had leased to them in the past. Carl wasn't just interested in the lease agreements, he was interested in everything related to them.

She looked at Bob. 'According to the lease we were just looking at, GES was supposed to pay Hart McConnell 12.5% of the sales from his lease, right?'

'I think those were the terms. Why?'

She pointed to the document open on her screen. 'Look at these figures. There were some months where he was owed at least $4500 but they only paid him $1100. That's a 75% difference.'

'It's not that uncommon,' replied Bob. 'Drilling companies are entitled to deduct fees from royalties. Just about everything hinges on that lease agreement and Mr. McConnell is probably some old-timer who didn't consult an attorney before he signed on the dotted line.'

Dana was appalled by the simplicity of it. 'It's greed, plain and simple.'

'I'm not disagreeing with you, sweetheart, I'm just saying how it is. There's a lot of money to be made in energy and energy companies are really good at making sure they get to keep most of it. As for the landowners, don't get caught up in feeling too sorry for them. That landman comes knocking on their door, promising to make them millionaires, and they like the sound of that just fine.'

She snorted at that. A landman's job was to acquire mineral rights for the lowest price while also getting as much control over those rights for their employer as possible. They were salesmen who were good at selling and, with rural communities struggling to survive, they had a captive audience.

She pushed the thought aside as she delved deeper into Carl's curious collection. And it was a collection, of people more than anything. Document after document, she noted the addresses, the names of towns, looking for associations. The properties identified in the lease agreements were near Alva, her father's hometown. A company like GES did business with landowners all over the state, all over the country. Why would Carl focus his attentions on this small section of Oklahoma?

But their proximity wasn't the only thing these landowners had in common.

'The landman in all these transactions is someone named Kevin Whitaker. Do you think that's significant?'

Bob sat up, his interest piqued. 'He's the landman in every case? Are you sure?'

'Positive. Why?'

'Kevin Whitaker is Karen's ex-husband. He was a big deal around here a few years back until all hell broke loose. He went from being the Golden Boy to being the man who had to pack his office in twenty minutes under the supervision of a security guard in the space of a day.'

She tried to imagine the man capable of wooing the indomitable Karen Forrester. Nothing sprang to mind. 'Where is he now?'

'Texas. New job, new house, new wife, new baby on the way.'

'Do you think it's possible Carl has some kind of beef with him?'

Bob shook his head. 'Kevin was long gone before Carl started working here. In fact, Carl was the first person Karen hired when she became the IT director here.'

Dana didn't bother to hide her confusion. 'So if Karen hired him, why didn't she also fire him?'

Bob shrugged. 'She protected Carl the same way I protected Bennie. It just so happened that Carl had a bad habit of abusing his privileges to access restricted files and he got caught one time too many with his hand in the cookie jar. Dean made the call, as usual, but Karen refused to cooperate so I had to be the bad guy.'

Things were beginning to fall into place. Carl was on a mission. If he couldn't get the job done as an employee, he would use the creptio spyware to do it for him. He was taking what he wanted.

'He's looking for something,' she declared. 'It's obvious he has a particular interest in this group of people. If it's not the landman connection, then it has to be the proximity.'

Bob motioned for her to trade places with him. It was like a game of musical chairs, except they took their chairs with them. Finally situated, he pushed his glasses up on his nose and studied the documents in earnest, absently rubbing his chin with his left hand. It was barely midnight and he already needed to shave.

After what felt like an eternity, he finally looked up. 'I agree with you about the proximity. It can't be a coincidence.'

She yawned. 'Is that it? They have nothing else in common?'

His eyes sparkled. 'You didn't actually read these documents, did you?'

'I scanned them.'

'These lease agreements are identical, sweetheart,' he said, letting her off the hook. 'Every last one of them.'

She wasn't sure she understood the significance. 'Is that bad?'

'It's the way these lease agreements are written,' he explained, 'It's basically a one-sided document that gives GES the right to do just about anything they want. They can deduct an undisclosed amount in fees from the royalty payments, there are no provisions for damage to property, crops, or animals, and there's nothing about providing an alternate source of water if the aquifer is contaminated. GES even retains the right to drill an injection well on the property if they want to.'

Dana knew that injection wells were a hot topic in the news. The wells were linked to an increase in seismic activity throughout Oklahoma, although she didn't know of a single drilling company who accepted the claim—at least not publicly. Drilling operations produced a lot of waste. Between the chemically treated water used in hydraulic fracturing and an abundance of naturally-occurring salt water, there was a lot to get rid of. Everyone agreed it had to go somewhere but that didn't mean they wanted it buried on their property.

'Is there such a thing as a predatory oil and gas lease?'

'There are some regulations in place to protect people but I think it mostly comes down to due diligence on the part of the landowner and whatever legal counsel they can afford.'

If she was honest with herself, she had to admit she was more confused now than she was when they started. Carl Payne was tearing up the GES network, not for trade secrets but for information related to chemical sales, environmental policies, and lease agreements with landowners in Northwest Oklahoma. There was no money to be made here, and, if there was, it certainly couldn't be enough to justify breaking and entering. It had to be personal.

An idea struck. She turned to Bob. 'Do you have access to personnel records?'

'Some, why?'

'I think I know what Carl is up to.'

Bob raised an eyebrow but he didn't argue. He logged into the GES personnel system and pulled up the record for Carl D. Payne, Status: Terminated. 'What do you want to know?'

'What's his address?'

'Oklahoma City. Looks like he lives off Britton Road.'

Dana swore. 'What about an emergency contact? Would GES still have that information?'

Bob click through a few screens. 'I'll be damned. His mother. Aileen Payne. Alva, Oklahoma.' He turned to look at Dana. 'You think he knows some of these people.'

'I think he's *related* to some of these people.'

Bob opened another application, a different database. He entered the name PAYNE in the search box. 'You may be on to something,' he agreed. 'We've got a Delbreth Payne in Woods County, Oklahoma.' He studied the screen with a frown. 'That's all we've got, though. For some reason, the file was never scanned into the system. And this code here,' he said, pointing to the screen, 'means the record is confidential. I can tell you right now the records clerk will never let us see it.'

It was almost laughable. Carl obviously didn't have access to this database or, if he did, he didn't know what he was looking at. What would he say when he found out he'd been dragging a net through the GES network for months for file that only existed on paper?

'That file is what Carl came here for.'

'Looks that way,' Bob agreed.

'We need to know what's in it.'

'We are *not* stealing this file,' he said resolutely. He cut her off when she tried to protest. 'But that doesn't mean we can't get the information,' he assured her. 'Alva's not that far. I can drive out there tomorrow and talk to a few people.'

'*You* can drive out there? What about me?'

He looked away. 'I don't think you want to come.'

'Of course I want to come. It was practically my idea.'

'It was my idea. And I don't think you do want to come along because I plan to take someone with me who knows the area and maybe even knows some of these families.'

He was being evasive, and she knew why. 'You're planning to take my father with you.'

'Yes.'

'And what makes you think he'll even agree to go with you on such short notice?' she challenged.

Bob smiled. 'He'll agree to go because you're going to ask him.'

Dana stared past the screen of her laptop through the large windows that faced the parking lot outside Bellwether Data Security. Being Saturday, the lot was mostly empty. The exposed blacktop was left to soften under the heat of the sun while everyone else went about their lives.

At least she had the office to herself. Even Floretta was absent for a change. The quiet soothed her. She was still reeling from this morning's conversation with her father. The exchange was strained, as usual, but he did manage to surprise her by agreeing to make the trip to Alva. She didn't know what his cooperation would cost her but she was sure he would think of something. For the moment, however, he was Bob's problem.

And so was Carl Payne. Whatever his motivation in all this, she was convinced he wasn't the only player on the field and she was no closer to understanding Bennie's movements in the days leading up to his death than she was a week ago. She had more suspects than she had crimes to match them with and too few answers all the way around. If the pieces were supposed to fit together, she had yet to see it.

She wasn't completely lost, however. There was still the little matter of Event B. Without the session key to decrypt the transmission, her client would never know what secrets they might have lost but that didn't prevent her from investigating who sent the data in the first place.

OpenSSH was a common find on a Linux box. System

administrators relied heavily on the Secure Shell protocol to remotely manage networked devices of every flavor. Conveniently, it could also be used as a tunneling protocol to provide end-to-end encryption between computer systems. Combined with the rsync utility also installed on the system, the server could be used to transfer files out of the company with great efficiency. If the culprit also managed to evade the firewall, no one would ever be the wiser.

Not surprisingly, the SSH config file showed signs of tampering. Someone configured the SSH server to listen on port 443 instead of its common port. It wasn't imaginative but at least it told her how the attacker was skirting the firewall.

Logging was disabled as well, as were passwords. Instead, authentication was accomplished using electronic keys. Either the perpetrator was concerned about security or had simply assumed control of an existing SSH server, pre-supplied with exploitable accounts. She guessed it was the latter.

A quick check of the authorized_keys file proved that there were several accounts authorized to establish an SSH connection with the server, probably for reasons that related to the server's original function. One of these accounts was responsible for the encrypted traffic they observed last night. It remained to be seen if she could isolate the account and connect it to an actual person but at least she had a place to start.

The account names didn't stand out. The naming convention seemed to be lastname.firstinitial but there were none she recognized. It was possible the employees who used the accounts no longer worked at GES. It wouldn't be the first time she'd encountered user accounts from a bygone era that should've been disabled but weren't. There *was*, however, something familiar about the authentication keys themselves. She had a memory for numbers and the long, alphanumeric strings reminded her of similar ones documented in Bennie's notebook.

Fortunately, the notebook and its translation were still bouncing around in her bag. Despite being a little worse for wear, they were intact enough to be useful.

Bennie's list of keys was quite lengthy, well beyond the scope of the handful of keys stored on this one server, but its length didn't hinder her search efforts. He'd accounted for all the keys she found but there was no mention of the server itself. In fact, the extent of his notes seemed to suggest Bennie was conducting a general audit of SSH keys period.

In the hands of a legitimate security professional, an audit like this could be used to strengthen the security posture of the network by weeding out old, unneeded accounts and keys. Considering Bennie's involvement, however, she was left to wonder if he wasn't on the hunt for something he could exploit. Either way, the clues were scarce.

She flipped through the pages of the notebook for inspiration. They were scattered with sketches, doodles mostly. In addition to an impressive lineup of superheroes, a thumb drive marked with the letters 'B.P.' was a common motif. It seemed like an odd thing to cram into the margins of a notebook. It struck her as more odd that she had yet to find its real-life counterpart. The only logical explanation was that she wasn't looking in the right place.

She fumbled around in her bag until she found Detective Mercer's business card. She'd plucked it out of her kitchen drawer the morning after she found the notebook but never bothered to dial the number because she didn't really have any solid leads. Technically, she didn't have any solid leads now but she did need a favor. She just hoped the man didn't mind working weekends.

Folks have a saying in Oklahoma: If you don't like the weather, wait five minutes and it'll change. Bob looked around at the dry, wind-swept fields flanking Highway 281 and decided that the changing weather around here must come with everything but the rain. His passenger agreed.

'It seems like it gets worse every year,' observed John Sorensen without looking away from the window.

Tall, lanky, and bookish, John looked exactly like the genius he was. Bob struggled to imagine how a world-renowned mathematician could emerge from this remote landscape that was more sky than earth but there was no denying the truth of it. Of course, he wasn't a pensive, gray-haired man back then. Bob knew the stories. In his youth, John was golden-haired, blue-eyed, and bright as a new penny.

John stirred. 'My daughter hasn't spoken to me in over two years.' Like most things, he stated it as fact. He was not a man who went looking for sympathy. 'You can imagine my surprise, then, when she called me out of the blue this morning to ask me to spend the day with you.' He turned to look at Bob's profile. 'Is there something I should know about the two of you?'

Bob shook his head. 'I'm not sure that's a fair question under the circumstances.'

John nodded but said nothing. He wasn't the defensive type, either. 'I want her to know that I'm sorry,' he said at last.

'It's been fifteen years, John. She knows you're sorry.'

'Then why won't she forgive me?' he pressed, his voice full of hurt. 'Why won't she speak to me?'

Bob never took his eyes off the road. 'Because some things are unforgivable. Some things we just put a fence around and we don't go there anymore.'

'I'm her father.'

'That usually makes it worse, not better.'

'So it's a stalemate then,' replied John, resuming his watch over the swiftly passing fields. 'I assume that's why Dana didn't join us?'

'She doesn't know the area like you do,' Bob hedged. 'She doesn't know the people.'

John quirked an eyebrow. 'You think I still know these people?' He laughed. 'It's been a lot of years, son. These little towns aren't what they used to be. And when you get to be my age, you run into more old friends in the obituaries than you do on the street.'

Bob had been wondering about that on the drive up. He vaguely remembered Dana saying her father was in his forties when she was born. John was already chair of the math department by the time he met Dana's mother and, in his own words, 'it was a long courtship.' Bob didn't doubt it. Based on everything he'd ever heard, Dana's mother was a vivacious professor of classics and a life-long lover of romantic literature. By comparison, John was a perfect square.

Still, if he was alive and kicking after all these years, surely there was at least one other person he knew out here who could tell them what they needed to know.

'There's a man out here, name of Hart McConnell. Do you know him?'

John nodded. 'If it's the same Hart McConnell I'm thinking of, then I knew him well. I graduated with his youngest brother.' He pointed to a dirt road about a half a mile away. 'If you turn left down that road, you'll run right into his old place. Don't expect too much, though. The man's in his nineties, if he's still living.'

John may be getting up in years, mused Bob, but there was nothing wrong with his memory. As promised, the red dirt road ran headlong into a narrow gravel drive. The rusted white mailbox even had 'McConnell' still painted on the side, which Bob took as a good sign.

The small farmhouse at the top of the drive was in dire need of repairs but it was charming all the same. There was a set of threadbare sheets billowing on the line and an old cellar door propped open near the house but no one came to greet them.

'I'll go knock on the door,' offered John.

After several raps on the screen door, a wiry, white-haired woman emerged from the cellar with an apron full of potatoes. She was just a slip of a woman, with a wrinkle on her face for every star in the sky, but she had a graceful step and a twinkle in her eye. Bob liked her immediately.

She caught sight of John and beamed. 'Well as I live and breathe! Johnny Sorensen, you come right over here and give me a hug.'

John did as he was bid. 'Hello Mabel. I was hoping I might see you today. Any chance Hart is still with us?'

Her smile softened. 'The Lord called him home this past February. He had that terrible pneumonia, you know.' She noticed Bob in his chair. 'Is this one yours? He sure is a big 'un.'

John laughed. 'Well, sort of. He belongs to my daughter, Dana. Do you remember Dana?'

'That little bitty thing? Course I do.' Mabel looked around the yard. 'Didn't you bring her with you?'

'Not today,' replied John. 'I actually brought Bob out here because he had some questions for Hart. I'm sorry he couldn't be here.'

Mabel smiled at some distant memory. 'Me, too, baby. Me, too. Now you boys go find a spot to sit down under that shade tree over there and I'll get us all somethin' cold to drink.'

She disappeared into the house with her potatoes and came striding back out with three Mason jars brimming with ice water. She handed Bob the first glass. 'So what was it you came here to ask?'

'I was hoping you could tell me about an oil and gas lease Hart signed several years ago.'

'Not much to tell,' she said matter-of-factly. 'We made some money on the deal—not as much as that man promised us, mind—but then the well ran dry and the company skedaddled. The checks stopped comin' and we ain't never heard from 'em since.'

Bob nodded. 'I was also wondering if you knew a man named Delbreth Payne. John doesn't know him but the lease had a local address on it.'

'Oh, Johnny wouldn't know him. It was after his time,' she explained. 'Del had the farm just up the way. I think they came here in the summer of 1970. Lives up in Ark City with one of his boys now, though. Moved up there when the bank took his farm.'

'He went bankrupt?'

'Oh, yes. He'd been strugglin' for years. It's a real common problem for folks out here. Cain't hardly grow nothin' in the dirt on account of no rain, cain't keep the livestock goin' when the water dries up, but you still got to pay your light bill on time. Some folks get money from them drillin' companies, and that helps, but it don't always work out. Del lost a water well 'cause of it. We did, too, but we were lucky. We were able to drill another one. It's not as close to the house as we'd like, of course, and the water ain't as sweet but it's better'n nothin'.'

'What did Del do for water?'

Mabel sighed. 'He tried to make do with a water tank for a while. He sold his cattle off and planted a few fields but the crop failed. He took a turn for the worse after that. Then his youngest boy came and got him and the bank got was was left. Not that it'll do 'em any good. What can you do with a piece of land without water when it don't rain?'

Bob pulled out his phone to take a note. 'You say he's with his youngest son? Do you happen to know how I can reach him?'

'Oh, I never got an address, honey, but the boy's name is Carl. Carl Payne. Seemed like a real good boy. His mama just lives over at Alva, you know. I always thought it was such a shame she and Del got a divorce when they did. They were both such sweet people.'

Dana looked up at the 55-foot glass sculpture that occupied the three-story atrium of the Oklahoma City Museum of Art. Light shone on the Eleanor Blake Kirkpatrick Tower 24-hours a day but she liked it best in the morning, before the crowds showed up. The column of glittering, meandering vines in yellow and gold and green and blue, more than 2000 blown-glass pieces in all, reached up to the sunlit sky in what could only be described as a fantastic display of optimism. She wouldn't mind having some of that optimism for herself right about now.

Detective Mercer slid up next to her, clad in street clothes. 'You sure picked an interesting place for us to meet.'

She shrugged. 'I like to come here to think.'

Mercer nodded, taking a moment to appreciate the magnitude of the sculpture towering over them. 'This is a good place for that,' he agreed, 'but I didn't get the impression on the phone that you wanted to discuss art.'

She turned to look at him. His blue eyes were unflinching. He may be a small man, she thought, but he had mettle. 'I want to have a look around inside Bennie Price's home. I think he may have a thumb drive that will help me understand what he was working on before he was killed.'

Mercer's eyebrows flew up. Whatever he was expecting her to say, that wasn't it. 'What makes you think he was killed?'

Dana opened her bag and pulled out Bennie's tattered notebook. 'This.'

Mercer took the notebook and flipped through the pages. He was intrigued but didn't know what to make of it. 'I assume you know what this says?'

'It doesn't tell you who his killer is, if that's what you're asking.' She gestured to the notebook. 'The only thing it really proves is that Bennie was digging in places where he wasn't welcome. I know it sounds crazy, but I think he discovered someone else's crime while he was busy trying to commit his own and he wound up paying for it with his life.'

Mercer stared at her, the wheels of his mind in motion. She couldn't tell if he was going to cooperate with her or if he was going to arrest her. Fortunately, he chose the friendlier option. 'If you want to take a look around his apartment, we'll go look, but we're not going anywhere until I get the whole story.' He pointed to the sign directing them to the museum cafe. 'Your treat.'

CHAPTER TEN

Answers

Bennie Price's apartment was stifling. Dust hung in the air as if suspended by some unseen aether while a plant wilted in a corner. Vintage comic books hung in frames over a worn, brown leather couch that loomed in the tiny living room opposite an equally tiny galley kitchen. The upper cabinets had no doors; the meager selection of dishes was disturbed, as if someone recently went through them.

Detective Mercer followed her gaze. 'That was us,' he explained. 'We were checking some of the glasses for fingerprints.'

She imagined the dishes in her own cupboards. No doubt they were covered in fingerprints, just like everything else she owned. 'Did you find any that weren't his?'

'One. Mr. Price died after ingesting a lethal dose of the drug alprazolam intensol mixed into a glass of whiskey.' He gestured to the couch. 'The glass was by him when he was found. We recovered his fingerprints from it along with a partial that doesn't belong to him.'

'Is that unusual? Maybe someone else handled the glass at some point in the past, like a friend or family member.'

'The glass was part of a set. Four double old-fashioned glasses, monogrammed with his initials, a gift from his parents. Two were in the back of the cabinet, covered in dust but obviously handled by him at some point. A third was spotlessly clean, no prints. The fourth was found next to his body.'

His meaning was clear. 'You think he wasn't alone that night,' she ventured. 'You think someone was here with him, someone who poured him a lethal cocktail and washed their own glass clean before they left him here to die.'

Mercer nodded. 'I actually think he was already dead when the person left. According to the medical examiner, Mr. Price would've been unconscious within minutes and dead within a half-hour. Forty-five minutes, tops.' Mercer pointed to various objects in the kitchen. 'Aside from the glass, there were other items that didn't yield any usable prints where we would expect to find them. The drug is a liquid, it uses a dropper. No prints on either the bottle or the dropper. The whiskey bottle was also clean. And what are the odds, do you think, of a person being able to write a suicide note without touching the paper?'

Dana hugged herself to avoid touching anything. 'I'm obviously not an expert but I don't see how anything you've just described could be construed as suicide. Where did that idea even come from?'

Mercer shrugged. 'There was a note. Aside from that, there were no witnesses. No suspects. No motive. No physical evidence to speak of. All I have is a handful of inconsistencies and a question in my mind. Medical examiners present facts, not ideas, and families want closure. If the truth can't be known, the tendency is to just make something up that fits all the pieces together.'

'Why didn't you tell me any of this before?'

'A fellow detective over in the white collar crimes unit told me that one of her contacts, the CIO of Grasslands Energy Solutions, had reached out to her,' he explained. 'She said he was asking questions about Bennie Price. When she told me he'd engaged the services of a consultant who also happened to be a licensed private investigator with an excellent reputation, I knew I'd caught a break.' He smiled, somewhat sheepishly. 'I didn't know how you'd be useful, exactly, I just knew you would be. I figured the best thing to do would be to introduce myself and let you go off and do your thing, whatever that is.'

She laughed in spite of herself. She certainly had 'done her thing.' And now she was standing in a dead man's apartment. 'I'll be sure to thank you for that one of these days,' she said as she stepped further into the living room. She could see a short hallway leading to a bedroom and a bathroom.

'And you might as well know that the licensed PI thing is mostly for show,' she added. 'Most of my colleagues are licensed, too. It's something juries like to hear when we take the stand and that means attorneys like it, too.'

Mercer smiled. 'Good to know. So what's this thumb drive we're looking for?'

'It's run-of-the-mill,' she replied absently as she mentally flagged the most suitable places to hide small objects. 'Black, marked with the initials B.P. in white. He probably used a white-out pen.' She pulled a pair of disposable gloves out of her back pocket and tugged them over her hands.

'You've done this before,' observed Mercer with approval before removing a pair of gloves from his own pockets.

'Yes, well, since I already told you about my PI license, I should probably also tell you that I usually do this sort of thing illegally.'

Mercer's eyebrows shot up but he said nothing. He searched the kitchen while she looked in the living room. It was a quick operation. She looked under every surface, behind every frame, between every crack, on every ledge. Nothing. A glance across the room at Mercer confirmed that he didn't find anything either. It was the same story in the bathroom. The bedroom, arguably the most personal room in anyone's home, was more interesting visually but still didn't offer much by way of ideal hiding spots.

Between them, they checked all the likely and unlikely places in the room and came up empty. Her last hope was an old shoe box wedged in the space between the headboard and the wall.

'Do you know what's in here?' she asked, sliding the box out into view. It was heavy.

'Rocks,' mumbled Mercer from the closet area. He was double-checking pockets.

Intrigued, Dana opened the box. Mercer wasn't kidding. It was a box of rocks. The kind of rocks you find, not the kind you buy.

Bennie's collection of Cherokee rose rocks was especially impressive. She wondered where he found them all. Her mother told her the legend of the rocks when she was a girl. She said they were formed from the blood of braves and the tears of maidens as they fell to the ground along the Trail of Tears. Her father told a different story, of course. He said they were barium sulfate crystals, as if they were so ordinary. But they weren't ordinary. Each rosette was millions of years old. To hold one in your hand was to hold millions of years of history. Dana liked to think that was almost as good as legend.

On impulse, she dumped the rocks out onto the floor. An envelope dropped out along with the stones. She gently pried the envelope open, half expecting to find a stash of emergency money but it turned out to be another collection, this time of photographs. Mercer, finished with his task in the closet, looked over her shoulder.

'Family photos,' he commented. 'Pictures of himself when he was a boy. Also a few photos of old girlfriends.'

Dana sifted through the pictures. 'Do men really keep pictures of old girlfriends?'

Mercer grinned. 'Some men do. And speaking of girlfriends,' he said, reaching into the top drawer of Bennie's dresser to reveal an article of lingerie, 'I don't suppose you have any idea who this might belong to?'

Dana quirked an eyebrow. It was an expensive piece, very elegant. 'He didn't have a girlfriend that I know of. Maybe it was his?'

'Men with that particular penchant usually have a dedicated drawer,' Mercer replied matter-of-factly.

She smiled at that and returned her attention to the photos. Poor Bennie. If these pictures were anything to go by, he was a sweet-natured, sentimental man. No matter how misguided his attempts might have been, he must have believed he was doing the right thing at GES. He certainly didn't deserve to die for it, if that's even why it happened.

One of the photos caught her attention. It was a selfie, taken in winter. Even with the hat and scarf, Dana instantly recognized the woman wrapped in Bennie's arms. And this was no friendly hug, either. This was a romantic embrace. They were a couple.

Mercer must have noticed the expression on her face. 'You know the woman in the photo?'

Dana hauled in a breath and stuffed the photo in the back pocket of her jeans. 'I need to borrow this picture, I promise I'll get it back to you soon.' She hurriedly dropped the rest of the photos back into the bottom of the box before standing to leave.

Mercer looked concerned. 'Why the rush?'

'I don't have time to explain. I have to get back to GES.'

'I don't understand,' said Mercer, frustration evident in his voice. 'Is this about the thumb drive or is this about the woman?'

Dana snapped off her gloves and strode for the door. 'Both, Detective Mercer. It's about both.'

Bob studied the photograph on his desk, obviously surprised by what he saw. 'I had no idea these two were ever in a relationship.

Bennie never said a thing about it. But that doesn't mean it was a secret,' he added. 'We didn't talk about stuff like this.'

'Maybe you didn't talk about it but I did. Ruby lied to me,' said Dana, still livid from the discovery. 'And if she lied about this then she could be lying about other things.' She snapped up the photo. 'I found this in Bennie's apartment, in a box of mementos. Whatever their relationship status was when he died, she obviously meant something to him. He would've trusted her enough to let her into his apartment, enough to let her help herself in the kitchen and pour them both a drink.'

Bob was unconvinced. 'Finding a photograph of someone in the apartment of a dead man doesn't make that person guilty of murder, even if they did lie about a relationship. And since when do you have a key to Bennie's apartment?' He sat bolt upright in his chair. 'You didn't use that stupid lock pick set to break in, did you?'

She arched a brow. 'What set would that be? The one you bought me?'

The look of horror on his face would've been amusing if not for the hypocrisy of it. She wondered if this was a good time to remind him that he was the one who was guilty of plotting against his own company, not her.

'I didn't break in,' she assured him. 'I was escorted by the homicide detective who's working Bennie's case.'

Bob couldn't have been more stunned if she'd slapped him. 'What are you talking about? What homicide detective?'

Dana dug Mercer's card out of her bag and handed it to him.

'Detective Richard Mercer. OKCPD. He stopped by my house shortly after I took this gig. He heard about my involvement in the case through your contact in the white collar crimes unit.'

Bob swore and raked a hand through his hair. 'You went behind my back?'

'I didn't go behind your back,' replied Dana hotly. 'Your contact went behind your back. It just so happens that something occurred to me this morning and I wanted to search Bennie's apartment so I called Detective Mercer, end of story. I would've included you but you were with my father at the time and I didn't want to wait.'

'That does not negate the fact that you should've told me about this a week ago.'

'I didn't trust you a week ago. I'm telling you now.'

Bob crossed his arms, his expression unreadable. 'Okay, then, tell me what you were looking for in Bennie's apartment.'

'A thumb drive marked with his initials. I noticed several sketches of it in his notebook and I thought it might be at his house. I think it's important to the case.' She grimaced. 'It wasn't there, of course, which is why I think we need to search Ruby's desk. If anyone would understand its significance out of context, I think it would be her.'

'We're *not* breaking into Ruby Hornbuckle's desk.'

'Why the hell not? She lied about her relationship with Bennie. He used her name as the encryption key for his secret diary for Christ's sake. She's involved in this somehow and you know it.'

Bob reached into his pocket to pull out a key ring. 'We're not going to search her desk because we don't need to. Your thumb drive is right here, in my desk.'

Now it was Dana's turned to be stunned. 'What?'

'I removed it from his office along with some notes shortly after I got word of his death,' he explained as he opened his desk drawer to pull out a pile of notebooks and papers held together with rubber bands. 'If someone found his notes and figured out what they were, I never would've been able to stick around to find out what happened to Bennie.'

'I'm sorry, weren't you just berating me for not telling you about Detective Mercer?'

Bob rolled his eyes. 'I would've given you the damn drive the very first day if I'd known it was that important.' He fished out the thumb drive and tossed it to her. 'What do you think is on it?'

She slipped her laptop out of her bag. 'Bennie was scrubbing the network, looking at all the SSH servers and clients he could find. He was using his privileges to assemble lists of authentication keys. I think he was foraging for vulnerabilities he could exploit to further your cause and inadvertently stumbled across something he couldn't explain. And then I think he got curious.'

'You think he found something that attracted the wrong kind of attention?'

'Yes, and whatever proof we have is probably on here,' she said, jamming the thumb drive into the side of her laptop.

Bennie, it turned out, had a few packet capture files of his own, and she doubted he used an inline tap to get them. He also had what looked to be a fairly comprehensive list of SSH keys.

Whatever else she might say about him, he was definitely thorough. It was a shame he didn't live long enough to rejoin the team at Bellwether. He would've been a good asset for the company.

She pointed to the screen. 'Look at the routing information on these packet captures. These transmissions were sent to the same IP address we saw with Event B.'

'Well, that would certainly explain Bennie's interest in SSH keys. Did he trace the source IP to a local user?'

'If he did, he didn't put it in writing. Not that it matters. The internal IP is not a match to the event we recorded.'

Bob swore. 'So it's possible Bennie didn't know who he was tracking. All he knew for sure was that something was going down, *something big.*'

Dana stared at the screen. It was a chilling thought but she couldn't deny the possibility. The whole situation reeked of industrial espionage and there was plenty of motive in that.

Bob interrupted her thoughts. 'We have to finish this. We need a name, a box, something.'

Dana clamped her eyes shut, forcing herself to focus. The IP addresses were a distraction, a wild goose chase waiting to happen. Bennie went to the trouble of cataloging authentication keys for a reason. That's where she needed to start.

SSH keys were better than passwords because they were generated as pairs. Two distinct, mathematically related numbers used for identification and authentication. Two interlocking keys that only opened doors when joined together.

In order for a client system to establish a secure connection with a server, it had to have the public key on file that corresponded to the server's private key and vice versa. Bennie already did the work for her. If she wanted to know if any two systems were communicating via SSH on the network, all she had to do was check to see which systems had each other's public keys.

Bob looked over her shoulder. 'Can I help?'

'I'm running a search. I'm comparing the authorized_keys file on the server to the known_hosts files Bennie harvested from GES systems. Wherever there's a match, there's a suspect.'

Bennie's organization paid off. Exactly two systems at GES had public keys that corresponded to Carl's server. Instead of IP addresses, however, Bennie documented computer names. This was useful because most companies developed naming conventions that made it easier for technicians to locate the systems quickly.

'Do you have any idea where these two systems are?' she asked.

Bob nodded, his expression grim. 'As a matter of fact I do. I know exactly where they are.'

Dana was worried. 'Do you want to tell me where we're going?' she demanded, lengthening her stride to keep up with Bob as he tore out of the elevator lobby.

He turned left at the first hallway, never slowing his pace. 'We're going to get answers.'

As soon as they rounded the corner, she knew exactly where he was taking her. 'These systems are in the IT department? How did Carl pull that off without being seen?'

He smiled grimly and inserted his key card into the reader at the IT entrance. 'He didn't.'

As soon as they were inside, they knew they weren't alone. Bob lifted his finger to his lips and Dana dropped to a crouch against the wall as he wheeled forward, following the sound. Moments later, he motioned for her to follow him down the hall, towards Bennie's office.

The harsh afternoon sun spilled in through the window, throwing light on the slender form bent over the desk. Dana's papers, mostly handwritten notes, were strewn everywhere. Bob rapped on the door loudly. Ruby, caught by surprise, spun around and shrieked. Documents fluttered out of her hands onto the floor.

Bob's tone was deadly. 'Would you like to tell me what you think you're doing in here, Ms. Hornbuckle?'

Ruby stood stock-still, shaking like a leaf. Dana almost felt sorry for her. She slid around Bob and dropped herself into the straight-backed chair across from Bennie's desk. 'Why don't you go ahead and have a seat, Ruby. I think we need to have a chat.'

Ruby looked to the door but clearly didn't like her odds of making it past Bob so she sank into the desk chair, her back ramrod straight.

Dana reached into her back pocket and produced the photograph. Ruby flinched when she saw what it was. 'You purposely misled me about the nature of your relationship with Bennie.'

'It wasn't your business.'

Dana nodded. 'I suppose that's true. Still, I wish you'd told me.

I wouldn't have subjected you to helping me pack Bennie's personal belongings if I'd known.'

Ruby looked down at her hands. Dana could see they were balled up in her lap. Any moment, tears would be streaming down her face.

'Where did you get that picture?' she whispered.

'From a box in Bennie's apartment.'

Ruby's head shot up. 'You were in his house?'

'Earlier today, as a matter of fact.'

'Who let you in?'

'A police detective.'

'So it's true?'

'What's true?'

'I took Bennie's work things to his parents this morning. They live out in the country,' she explained. 'They got a call while I was there. Someone from the police asked permission to re-enter Bennie's apartment. I didn't understand what was going on. I don't think his parents did, either—not entirely—but they said there's a detective who thinks Bennie's death might not have been suicide so they figured he wanted to look around again.'

Ruby's face was swollen and wet with tears, her shoulders rolled forward in defeat. Dana didn't know how she figured into this mess but she was definitely no murderer. Bob, apparently coming to a similar conclusion, relinquished control of the door and offered her a clean handkerchief, which she accepted.

'So let me see if I understand this,' pressed Dana. 'You find out that Bennie may have been the victim of foul play and you make a bee line for this office. Why?'

'A few days ago, you said you found some of Bennie's old notes. You were asking me about them.'

'You came here looking for his notes?'

Ruby nodded.

'And what did you expect to find?'

Ruby shrugged. 'I don't know. What happened to him, I guess.'

'What did you think happened to him? Before this morning, I mean.'

Ruby gripped the handkerchief in her hand, no longer bothering to sop up her tears. 'I did something,' she whispered. 'But I had to do something,' she insisted. 'He wouldn't tell me what it was but I knew something was wrong, especially by the end. Things had gotten so tense between us. He was working late, he was secretive, he would hardly talk to me. Karen had her claws into him bad. I had to do something,' she sobbed. 'But then, but then—'

'Then he killed himself,' offered Dana gently.

'But maybe he didn't,' said Ruby, hope in her voice. 'That's what that cop thinks. He thinks Bennie didn't kill himself at all. I remembered what you said about Bennie's notes, that you didn't understand them, and I knew I could figure it out. We had a special shorthand that we'd use sometimes, kind of a secret code. He liked to make up word games and then he'd let me try to solve them. We did it all the time.'

Dana hauled in a breath. She'd had a niggling suspicion that

Bennie used HORNBUCKLE as the encryption key for a reason, perhaps even to point a finger at his would-be killer. She was right about the key's significance but wrong about everything else. Ruby was telling the truth about the word games. Bennie probably encrypted his most sensitive notes to protect them from prying eyes, but then things went sideways. She could see it now. Bennie, realizing the gravity of his discovery, gets down on hands and knees to tape the notebook under his desk as a precaution. No matter what happened, he knew he could always count on Ruby. It was an insurance policy he didn't know he needed, and it just so happened that Dana got there first.

Bob rolled forward. 'Dana is also very good at word games, she already decoded Bennie's notes. She's been helping to solve Bennie's murder since she got here.' He grabbed a box of Kleenex off the edge of the desk and handed it to Ruby. 'It would help us a lot if you'd tell us everything you know, starting with whatever it is that you think you did to cause Bennie to commit suicide.'

Ruby dried her eyes and sat up a little straighter. Realizing she was in a room with allies seemed to give her strength.

'Bennie was, um, *doing things*. On the network, I mean. Things he wasn't supposed to be doing. It was kind of a special project. I wasn't supposed to know about it,' she admitted, 'but he couldn't keep things from me.' She halted, new tears forming in her eyes from some distant memory but she managed to mop them up before they slid down her face.

'But then Bennie told me he wanted us to take a break. He said things were moving too fast. I figured out there was another woman but he always denied it. And then I saw them together. It was an accident, I wasn't supposed to see. He asked me to keep it a secret. And I did keep his secret but I knew she was just using him. And then things got weird, just like I said. I had to do something.' She held back a sob and took a deep breath.

'I knew she wouldn't want him if he didn't work here anymore, so I reported him to management. I told them about the things he'd been doing on the network so there'd be an investigation. I knew he'd get fired. And it seemed like it worked, he even had another job lined up already. But then he didn't show up for work, which was strange because it was almost his last day. We had a cake in the conference room for him and everything. And then later they came in and told us that, well, that he, that he—'

'You don't have to say it,' said Bob, grief palpable in his voice. 'We know what happened next. So you turned him in to drive a wedge between him and a woman. What woman?'

'He was having an affair with Karen Forrester,' she whispered. 'But nobody was supposed to know.'

They sat in stunned silence for a full minute before Bob spoke. 'You said you knew she was using him. Do you know how she was using him?'

Ruby shook her head. 'I'm sorry, I don't. I just figured there had to be a reason for a woman like that to be so interested in Bennie. He wasn't that kind of man. He was too good for someone like her.'

Dana stood up. She pulled Richard Mercer's card out of her bag and handed it to Ruby. 'I want you to go home now and have a bath. And then I want you to call this detective and tell him everything you just told us.'

A few minutes later, Dana watched Ruby climb into her car and drive off from Bennie's window. 'Poor girl. It's so obvious she was in love with him. I don't know how anyone could compete with a woman like Karen, though. Smart, beautiful, and sophisticated is a tough combination to beat, even if she does come up short in the personality department. And Ruby's right. If Karen had an interest in someone like Bennie, there had to be a reason.' She thought of the expensive lingerie in Bennie's drawer. 'Do you think it was the sex?'

'I think was more than that,' said Bob. 'A lot more. You know those two computer names we came looking for?'

Dana nodded.

'What would you say if I told you they were both in Karen's office?'

Bob flung open the door to Karen's office with considerably more force than was needed. His blood surged through his veins, his brain overflowed with competing signals. His body wanted to stand, to kick the wall in, to run out of the building with reckless speed, but his brain, try as it might, couldn't make it happen. He would never walk again and neither would Bennie. Trouble is, he was beginning to doubt whether it even mattered anymore. Of all the possibilities to enter into his mind since the moment he learned of Bennie's death, the one thing he never thought of was that Bennie may have gotten just what he deserved.

Dana was careful to leave space between them but she knew what was on his mind. 'You think Bennie is involved, don't you?'

'Don't you?' he challenged. 'You're right about Karen. If she went after Bennie, it was for a reason. And if she had him in her sights, he never stood a chance.'

She quirked an eyebrow. 'If I didn't know better,' she ventured, 'I'd say you were speaking from experience.'

'What was it you said? Smart, beautiful, and sophisticated?' He smiled bitterly. 'Well, she is definitely all of those things. She's also opportunistic, devious, and manipulative. More importantly, she's not you. In what I can only describe as an extraordinary lapse in judgment, I allowed myself to be drawn into her snare. Just the one time, thank God, but she's been holding it over my head ever since.' He shook his head. 'All this time, Bennie was mixed up in one of her schemes and I didn't have a clue.'

'How could you know?'

'How could I not know?'

Her expression was taut, unreadable. 'Oh, I think you'd be surprised. People are better at hiding things than you might think.'

He knew she wasn't talking about Bennie. If he was honest with himself, he knew she wasn't talking about him, either. Her pain went back much further than that, back to a time when she was a different person, bound for a life that never would've crossed his path.

He cleared his throat and moved into position behind Karen's desk. 'Well, if that's the case, then let's have a look at what Karen's been hiding.'

There wasn't time to work with forensic images. The best they could manage was to use write blocking software to inspect the contents of both hard drives without making any inadvertent modifications. He wasn't surprised by their findings. They already knew what Karen was up to, all they needed was proof. And, whether she knew it or not, she left more of that lying around than any court could ever need.

Dana was fishing around in Karen's file cabinet. 'Look at this,' she said, holding up Bennie's jacket. 'There's also a framed photograph in here. It's a picture of them together at his apartment.'

He snorted. 'Good. Your detective friend is going to need every piece of evidence he can get to tie her to the scene of Bennie's death.'

She dropped the jacket back into the drawer. 'Wasn't it you who said a photograph wasn't enough to prove murder?' She frowned. 'I can't help but think we're missing something here. Why would she keep mementos like this?'

'I think you're mistaking souvenirs for mementos. She's a sociopath. Why wouldn't she keep trophies?'

Dana was unconvinced. 'At her office? She's smarter than that, babe.'

His task with the hard drives completed, he searched the desk. Aside from a surprising amount of junk food, there was nothing out of the ordinary. The only thing left was a small decorative box next to the desk lamp. Unfortunately, it was locked.

He was picking at the lock with a paper clip when Dana tossed a file folder down in front of him. 'Here,' she said, reaching for the box. 'Let me do that. I think you'll want to see what's in that file.'

He handed the box to Dana gladly. She was the better lock pick by far. The file, it turned out, contained two documents. The first was a printout of access codes for the data center and Ruby Hornbuckle's name was circled in red ink; the second was a draft memo alerting the GES Board of Directors that Karen possessed evidence connecting Kevin Whitaker with acts of industrial espionage—and, furthermore, she recommended the board contact the FBI on the matter.

'Holy shit.' It was all he could say.

Dana grinned. 'I know. I thought it was an old memo at first, that it might be the reason why Kevin Whitaker was terminated so quickly, but look at the letterhead. Your company has been using that logo for less than a year.'

Bob was impressed. The new logo was part of a shift in the company culture. GES had been transitioning from drilling to technology for years but they'd only made it official recently. 'How the hell could you possibly know that?'

'After all the time I spent pouring over documents in Bennie's office? It didn't take me long to figure it out.'

He marveled at her attention to detail until her meaning sunk in. Kevin was a schemer but there was no way he was in cahoots with his scheming ex-wife. 'She's setting the bastard up.'

There was a distinctive click as Dana finally popped the lock open. She gasped when she lifted the lid.

'Well, what is it?' he asked, impatient to see its contents.

Dana held a ring aloft. A bold sapphire, ringed with diamonds, mounted on a gold band. His grandmother's ring.

'She wasn't anywhere near the server room last night,' said Dana, wrapping her fingers around the ring protectively. 'The only person who could've given her this was Carl.'

Alarm bells went off in his head. If she was working with Carl and not Bennie, then she'd have more than enough motive to kill Bennie the second she found out he was on to her. 'We need to lock this place down and call the police,' he said, reaching into his pocket for his cell phone. He swore violently. Of all the times to leave his phone on his damn desk. Karen's didn't have a land line, she used VoIP software and a headset.

He wheeled around the desk and pushed Dana toward the door. They'd just have to make the call from somewhere else. She was mid-protest when the voice he dreaded to hear sounded from the hallway.

Karen's form loomed tall. She was holding a handgun and, if he knew Karen, it was loaded. She smiled sweetly. 'What's the hurry? It seems a little rude to rush off when I just got here, don't you think?'

CHAPTER ELEVEN

Game Over

Dana eyed Karen's pistol, a .22 caliber in basic black. Her grip on the weapon was relaxed, as was her stance, but Dana suspected both were subject to change.

Satisfied she had their attention, Karen edged further into the room. 'Now, which one of you wants to tell me what the hell you're doing in my office?'

Bob wheeled forward, apparently unfazed by the presence of a weapon. 'You can put the gun down, Karen. It's not what you think. We're here investigating a murder.'

It was hardly subtle but then Bob didn't tend to be subtle. Dana just hoped he had a plan.

Karen arched an elegant brow, clearly amused. She lowered her weapon. 'And whose murder would that be?'

'Bennie Price.'

Her expression faltered. 'You're lying.' She leveled her gun again, this time on Bob. 'Why are you really here?'

'He's telling the truth, Karen.'

'I suggest you mind your own business, Ms. Sorensen. As I recall, you don't even work here.' She looked at Bob. 'Everyone knows Bennie Price committed suicide.'

'The medical examiner begs to differ,' interrupted Dana. 'And so does the OKCPD.'

Karen wavered. Even she couldn't deny the truth when she heard it. The nose of the gun dipped. 'If what you're saying is true, then why are you snooping around in here?'

'As if you didn't know,' spat Bob. 'You know full well that Bennie was on to your little scheme with Carl Payne.'

She blanched.

'What's the deal with Carl anyway?' he asked. 'Did you promise him the opportunity to avenge his father in exchange for services rendered?'

Judging by the look on Karen's face, he'd hit the nail on the head.

But he wasn't finished. 'Just tell me one thing, Karen. Why Bennie? He wasn't a threat to you. The damn fool was probably in love with you.'

'I don't know what you're talking about.' Surprisingly, her eyes welled with tears. 'I would never do anything to hurt Bennie, I cared for him. I had no idea he was investigating what Carl and I were doing.'

Dana was thrown by the sudden display of emotion but not fooled. 'Do you honestly expect us to believe that?'

'Believe what you want to believe,' seethed Karen. 'You didn't know Bennie like I did. He would've understood what I was doing, why I was doing it. You think I don't know what he was up to on the network, his little scheme with Bob? I stayed out of his way, he would've stayed out of mine.'

'You're wrong,' insisted Bob. 'Unlike you, Bennie didn't have a selfish bone in his body. He would never condone what you're planning. Do you realize that Kevin could wind up in prison if you succeed in framing him for industrial espionage? You do understand the concept of prison, don't you? You're not just going to ruin his life, you're going to ruin the lives of everyone around him. And for what? Petty revenge?'

Tears spilled down Karen's face. 'You think you know me? You don't know a goddamned thing about me.' She shook her head. 'And you don't know Kevin Whitaker, either. You don't know what he's really like behind closed doors. You don't know what he did to me.' She wiped her face using the back of her free hand. 'He's already done more than enough to spend the rest of his life in jail, I'm just helping the process along. And all those people around him? Those people you're so worried about? They'll be *safer* when he's behind bars.'

Bob opened his mouth to speak but closed it again, clearly at a loss for words. He didn't like Karen but Dana knew he liked men like Kevin Whitaker even less.

Karen was gripping her gun tightly now, Dana thought she detected a slight tremble in her hands. Things couldn't continue down this road for long.

'Let's say we believe you,' she suggested. 'We know someone hurt Bennie, someone he trusted. If not you, then someone else.

Can you think of anyone who might be threatened by what he was doing here?'

Karen blinked and finally lowered her gun. She shook her head. 'I don't know. That jealous little brat Ruby turned him in but I don't think she'd actually hurt him.' She gestured to Bob. 'And Bob couldn't hurt anybody.'

'What about Carl?'

That earned another raised brow. 'Carl? No. He's completely harmless. The only reason he's involved is because he wants to help his father. His father is very ill,' she explained. 'He didn't know his water well was contaminated until it was basically too late. GES was willing to settle with the old man but only if he signed a non-disclosure agreement. He refused, and, thanks to my ex-husband, the man was guaranteed to die of old age before he'd get anywhere in court so Carl took matters into his own hands. I was angry when I found out what he was up to but then I realized he and I could help each other. You know the rest.' She shook her head. 'Carl may be determined but he's not who your looking for.'

'What about your father?' ventured Bob.

'My father?' Karen almost laughed. 'I'll be the first to admit that he'll never win a man of the year award but he's no murderer. Believe me, if my ex-husband still draws breath after what he did, there's no way my father would do anything to Bennie. Besides, he didn't even know Bennie existed until Sam turned him in. Bennie was fired for his sins, my father was content with that.'

'It was Dean, not Sam, who went after Bennie,' corrected Bob.

'Oh, forgive me for insulting your precious mentor, I forgot the two of you were so close. But you're wrong. That stupid little twerp, Ruby, went running off to Sam weeks ago and Bennie knew it. And Bennie, by the way, was such a good guy that he didn't even hold it against her. Sam, on the other hand, well, he couldn't wait to sink his teeth into Bennie.'

'You're lying,' spat Bob.

Karen dropped the gun into her purse and pulled out her cell phone. She tossed it to Bob. 'Why not just call Ruby and ask? I dare you.'

'Enough!' boomed a voice from the doorway.

Sam Porter came into view. He came bearing a grim expression and a handgun to rival Karen's. If not for Bennie's murder looming in her mind, Dana could almost imagine she was in a Wild West radio show.

Moving with a speed not normally attributed to a man of his size, Sam snapped the phone out of Bob's hands and divested Karen of any idea she might have had to reach for her own gun. He was in charge of what happened next and they all knew it.

Sam leveled a harsh stare on Bob. 'I thought I told you not to let Ms. Sorensen out of your sight. She was here to do a job, not go gallivanting all over tarnation, sticking her nose into things. Stupid boy.'

'What the hell's going on, Sam?' demanded Bob. His confusion was palpable.

'Enough talking,' ordered Sam. 'The four of us are taking a walk and I don't want to hear another word. Now,' he said, pointing to the open door with gloved hands. 'March. And don't be thinking about hollerin' for help. No one's here to hear you.'

Bob stared at the access panel outside the data center, debating how cooperative he should be at this point. Sam wasn't talking, he wasn't even making eye contact. And now he was sending them into a windowless room with only one exit. Bob was liking their odds less and less.

Somewhere behind him, Dana sucked in a breath. He didn't need to turn around to know Sam was digging his gun into the small of her back. The message couldn't be clearer, do it or she dies. Bob punched in his code and swung the door wide.

Sam let the door fall shut behind him. The silence was deafening.

At length, he spoke. 'Do you know what the worst thing is about war?' He looked to where Bob sat in the center in the room and to Dana, who stood nearby. 'Collateral damage.'

Bob looked up at his old friend. 'Are we at war?'

'We're always at war, son. Against our competitors, against the lawyers, against the legislators, against the Environmental Protection Agency, hell, sometimes we're even at war with each other. Isn't that right, Karen?'

Karen was hugging herself, her delicate mouth locked in a thin line. She said nothing.

'Cat got your tongue?' taunted Sam. She flinched. 'This is your fault,' he informed her. 'You and that damn boyfriend of yours, gettin' up to no good, thinkin' you could just come in here and help yourself. I got news for you, little girl, this company doesn't owe you a goddamned thing.' His voice was venom. 'Did you think there wouldn't be consequences? Did you think we'd just let you go on undermining our operations? Did you?'

Sam didn't wait for a response as he inspected the inside door lock. After a moment of consideration, he slammed his gun into it. Pieces of the lock scattered to the floor. Some rolled away, falling into the space beneath their feet.

He rounded on Karen again. 'Did you know I started out in this business as a roustabout? That's how I spent my summers all through college. I learned everything I know from the ground up. That's how your father and I built this company. But you don't know anything about that, do you. You grew up with one of them silver spoons in your mouth and never thought a thing about where it came from. I bet there's a lot you don't think about.' He tapped on the busted lock mechanism. 'For one thing, you probably have no idea that this door lock is fail-secure. That means you won't be able to get out once I lock you in.'

Bob stared at the bits of plastic and metal on the floor. Sam didn't disable the lock, he disabled the emergency egress feature. The son of a bitch was setting a trap. He could feel Dana standing near him. Her body was tense, she was poised for a fight.

He pushed forward. 'You don't need to do this, Sam,' he reasoned. 'They can't throw you in jail without evidence and we don't have any to offer. It would be our word against yours and you have a dozen attorneys at your disposal.'

'I'm not here to avoid jail, son, I'm here to save the company I helped to create from ruin. It seems Karen here thought she was gonna teach her ex a lesson. I guess she was gonna make him out to be some kinda *industrial spy*. Well, he's some kinda somethin' alright.' He looked at Karen with disgust. 'What do you think of extortion, Karen? 'Cause that's what your ex is getting away with right now. Turns out you didn't do as good a job as you thought of hiding them files on his computer.'

Karen's face went white.

'Your ex drives a hard bargain, I'll give him that. His silence cost us a pretty penny. And then you went and left me a mess to clean up on top of it. I knew you had help, of course. No matter how smart you think you are, you'd need help for something like that. And that Bennie Price sure was a sneaky little shit. When he started coming around to my office real regular-like, I didn't figure it was for nothin'. It wasn't too long before that little girl told me what he was doing on our network and I knew I had my man. He was easy enough to deal with. I didn't even have to send the boys in—I was able to take care of it myself. Your little boyfriend drifted right off in his sleep before he ever knew a thing.'

He stalked up to Karen. 'I hoped it would stop with Bennie but I should've known you'd be too greedy for that.' He wagged a finger at her. 'I knew something was up when I started seein' that mouse racin' across my screen again and Ms. Sorensen here was kind enough to confirm my suspicions. You're like one of them addicts, you just don't know when to stop. Trouble is, this time it's gonna cost me a lot more than money. Your ex has made that abundantly clear.'

Bob wheeled forward, forcing Sam to look him in the eye. He

had to get Dana out of here. 'If you want to blame someone, Sam, blame me. If I'd been doing my job, none of this would've happened. You can do whatever you want with me, you can even have Karen but, for Christ's sake, let Dana go. She has *nothing* to do with this.'

Sam's expression was pained. 'I'm sorry, son. Dean and I worked too hard. We made too many sacrifices and invested too much money. The stakes are higher than you can imagine—I can't afford to be sentimental. Karen's been judged and this is her sentence. And since the two of you insisted on sticking your nose in, it's your sentence, too.'

He pointed to a pull station near the door. Bob recognized it as part of the aging halon fire suppression system he'd been trying to replace since he was first hired on as CIO. Aside from being damaging to the ozone layer, halon was generally hazardous to humans. The halon in use at GES was more than hazardous, it was deadly. If Sam manually activated the system and locked them in, they would run out of oxygen in a matter of minutes.

'You'll never get away with this,' Bob warned.

'It'll be your fingerprints they find, not mine. Your security code, too. You people are gonna do so much damage trying to get outta here, they'll assume it was all a terrible accident.'

Bob couldn't remember feeling so desperate. Dana was trembling. 'Sam, please don't do this,' he pleaded. 'Sam—'

They were out of time. Sam fled the room as halon gas began pouring in. Bob grabbed for the door handle but didn't manage to catch it before it locked. He beat the door with all his might. His upper body strength was considerable but he was no match for the solid wood door.

Out of the corner of his eye, he could see Dana searching the walls for a telephone. Karen, having finally returned to her senses, was attempting to disengage the halon system. Neither woman was having much luck. Even if Dana found a land line, help would never arrive in time.

His heartbeat was racing. He couldn't tell if it was the chemical or if it was fear. He grabbed at Dana as she darted past. 'We need to get this door open.' He pointed to a fire extinguisher on the wall. 'Grab that and use it on what's left of the lock. As fast and as hard as you can, sweetheart.'

Dana obeyed. She pounded the base of the fire extinguisher into the lock while he put every ounce of energy he had into forcing the door open. The wood creaked under the strain but refused to give.

His throat and eyes burned, his thoughts were muddled. The fire extinguisher dropped from Dana's hands as she collapsed into him. 'I can't do it,' she sobbed. 'I just can't do it.'

He gathered her close, ignoring the dull pounding in his head. 'You did your best, sweetheart, you did your best. It's all gonna be okay.' She was losing consciousness, he could feel it. He smoothed her hair away from her forehead and planted soft kisses on her cheeks. 'I love you, sweetheart,' he whispered. 'Always and forever.'

Dana stirred in his arms and managed to smile up at him before going completely limp. Her life was slipping away, his was not far behind. The pounding grew stronger, he wondered at the loudness of it as his eyelids dropped shut.

He never saw the door burst open. He was barely aware of the powerful arms that lifted him out of his chair. His last waking memory was of a patch of gray carpeting, which struck him as an odd color for heaven. But, then again, maybe it just meant that he'd ended up in hell after all.

Floretta was alone in her office when Dana knocked. She waved Dana in without looking up from her computer. Dana held back a smile. There was a part of her that would miss these little snubs.

She slid into one of the narrow chairs across from Floretta. 'There's a note on my desk that says your looking for me.'

Floretta finally looked up. 'I didn't expect to see you back here until tomorrow. Are you sure you're okay?'

'What? Am I witnessing an actual expression of *concern*?

'Well at least we know your sense of humor is intact,' countered Floretta as she slid a folder in Dana's direction.

Dana shoved it back the other way. She was done with folders. 'We're not doing this again, Flo. The answer is no.'

'It's not a case, you ninny. It's something I thought you should hear from me first. This scandal with GES is all over the news and we've already received a letter from their attorneys telling us they plan to sue over your involvement. They are citing breach of confidentiality,' she explained.

Dana snorted. 'If they think they can make it stick, more power to them. You're welcome to fire me if you think it'll make them feel better.'

'I could,' Floretta agreed, 'if not for the fact that you already took care of that yourself. Jeremy, by the way, was damn-near apoplectic when he found out you turned him down flat and then waltzed your ass downstairs to hand in your resignation on the same day.'

Dana smiled at that. She'd have to make a point of stopping by his office to say goodbye.

'Did you get my email?' she asked, changing the subject. 'The one I sent you about a girl named Ruby Hornbuckle?'

Floretta nodded. 'I did. I gather you think I should hire her despite the fact that she is wholly unqualified.'

'I wasn't qualified when you met me.'

'You had a math degree from Princeton University,' Floretta reminded her. 'This girl went to the local vo-tech.'

'If you pair her up with the right mentor, I think you'll be pleasantly surprised with what you get.'

'Alright, I'll give her a call. But I can't make any promises. In the meantime, I'd like to know when you were planning to tell me about your impending departure.'

'Well, that depends on when you were planning to tell me about yours.'

Floretta's eyebrows hit the ceiling. Dana basked in the moment. It was a rare day at Bellwether Data Security when Floretta Pickens was caught by surprise.

'So Jeremy told you about that, did he?'

'Was it a secret? If so, someone needs to tell Max.'

Floretta laughed. 'I'm not too worried about him, baby girl. In fact, he should be sitting down with Jeremy today to discuss his new salary.'

Now it was Dana's turn to be surprised. 'Max isn't your replacement?'

'Max Chen was never in the running for this job, although I know it would hurt his feelings terribly if he ever found out.'

'So does that mean you're staying?'

Floretta shook her head. 'I'll be out that door quicker than a shot once my successor is named. I might get out of here a little faster if you withdraw your resignation. If you play your cards right, you could be sitting in this chair by Christmas.'

'I appreciate the not-actually-an-offer, Flo, but I'm afraid I must respectfully decline. I turned my files and equipment over this morning,' she explained, rising from her seat. 'As soon as I walk out that door, you'll never see me again.'

'What if it was an actual offer?'

'Is it an actual offer?'

'Yes.'

'Then my answer is an actual no.'

Floretta grinned. 'Good for you, baby girl. Good for you. Now get the hell out of my office. And tell Bob to send me his resume. Oh, and Dana?' she called out just as Dana reached the door, 'I want you to know you're the best employee I ever had.'

As compliments went, it was about as good as she'd ever get. It was time she gave one of her own. 'If I was an excellent employee, Floretta, it was only because I had an excellent teacher.'

Bob was waiting for her outside with a bouquet of flowers. 'You'll never guess who just called me,' he said, holding the flowers out to her. 'Andy Paulson. He got hired on at a top notch security firm, he starts on Monday. He's pretty sure your recommendation landed him the job.'

Dana smiled and accepted the flowers. 'He's sweet for saying that but he didn't need my recommendation. He hurtled his body at a solid oak door to save the lives of three unconscious people. I'd say that's recommendation enough.' She dropped a light kiss on Bob's cheek. 'Thank you for the flowers. Floretta wants you to send her your resume, by the way. I think she wants you to be the new her.'

He laughed. 'We'll see if she still thinks that once Detective Mercer is done with me.'

'For the last time, it's not an interrogation,' she said, leading the way to the car. She parked in guest parking so it was a short walk. 'He just needs us to make an official statement.'

'So you think he'll overlook the fact that I didn't take my suspicions to the police?'

'Your suspicions were implied when you hired me.'

Bob lifted himself into the passenger seat and pulled his legs in while Dana stowed his chair. 'So have you heard from your contact at the OKCPD about how things are going with the case?' she called from behind the trunk.

'You mean you haven't been talking to Mercer?'

'No, he's busy. Besides, I knew I'd see him today.'

'Well, Sam's not talking. He's got some of the best lawyers in the country working for him but I understand Mercer has a rock solid case against him. Whether he likes it or not, Sam is going to jail for a very long time. Still no word on whether they'll be able to pin anything on Dean, though.'

She closed the trunk and settled into the driver's seat, turning the A/C on full blast. 'Poor Karen. How's she doing?'

'She's out of the hospital. She and Carl are cooperating fully. There's no way they'll get off clean but they both have good attorneys so who knows? At least they won't be going away empty handed.'

'How do you mean?'

'Kevin Whitaker is being brought up on extortion charges and, thanks to Carl's pioneering efforts, some of his past activities as a landman are coming under considerable scrutiny as well.'

'So Karen and Carl both get their revenge after all. I wonder what we're supposed to get out of this? Other than unemployment, I mean.'

Bob held out a small box. 'I thought you'd never ask.'

She took the jewelry box with nervous hands, forcing herself not to tear it open. Just as she hoped, a dazzling sapphire was nestled inside. It was his grandmother's ring, freshly cleaned and strung on a delicate gold chain.

'Mercer helped me get it back,' he explained as she undid the clasp and put it around her neck. 'It looks good on you,' he said appraisingly. He reached for her hand and pressed a kiss on the inside of her wrist. Her pulse jumped. 'So,' he ventured, 'what are my chances of getting you to wear that ring on your finger, the way nature intended?'

She snorted and leaned over to give him another peck on the cheek before strapping on her seatbelt. 'About the same as your chances of having sex with me.'

Bob laughed. 'Well, in that case, I'd say my chances are excellent.'

EPILOGUE

'Oh, let's look at this one next,' said Dana excitedly, waving an envelope in the air. 'It's from Mazie.'

Bob wheeled himself gingerly around the boxes stacked all over the floor to take the envelope. Unlike most of the notes and cards they'd looked at so far, this one was bright and filled with confetti. 'Congratulations on your new partnership,' he read.

'She sent us a bottle of champagne, too. It's in the fridge. Should I get it out?'

'Why not?,' said Bob, brushing confetti off his lap. 'I'd rather celebrate than unpack any day.'

Dana smiled. She was beautiful, even with her hair pulled up in a pony tail, wearing cut-off jeans, a pair of weathered Chuck Taylor's, and a t-shirt announcing to the world that All Spiders Eat Soup. She was glowing with excitement. He couldn't remember seeing her this happy, not even before the accident.

He popped the cork on the champagne while she fetched a sleeve of paper cups from under the sink of the tiny kitchenette. 'What shall we drink to?' he asked.

'To Sorensen & Leroy Information Security Services,' she announced, bumping her cup against his. 'Oh!' she added, 'we should also drink to Mazie. She takes over as the new Floretta on Monday.'

'To Sorensen & Leroy, and to Mazie,' said Bob, before taking a sip. It was cold and sweet and bubbly. 'So if Mazie is the new Floretta then where is old Floretta?'

Before Dana could answer, there was a rustle behind a pile of boxes, followed by a loud obscenity. Apparently, their uninvited guest stubbed a toe. Bob almost dropped his cup when Floretta came bursting forth with a box in hand.

'Don't ever let me hear you use the words *old* and *Floretta* in the same sentence again, Bob Leroy.' Floretta looked around their new offices with approval. She spotted the champagne and set the box on the floor. 'I hate to tell you this,' she said, pouring champagne for herself into an empty cup, 'but you people can't be sittin' around drinkin' at ten in the morning if you want to earn any money at this endeavor.'

Bob laughed and threw his arms wide to the chaos that surrounded them. 'I hate to burst your bubble, Flo, but this is hardly a money-earning endeavor. We just got the walls painted yesterday.'

Floretta snorted inelegantly, pressing a piece of paper into Dana's hand. 'It looks like I arrived at just the right time then.' She pointed at the piece of paper. 'That's your first paying customer right there. Don't agree to a penny less than $5000 for what he's asking. And you two best get a move-on, too, because you need to be there in an hour.' She looked around some more. 'So where am I supposed to sit?'

Bob had no idea what was happening but suspicion bloomed on Dana's face. 'What's in the box, Flo?' she asked.

Floretta reached into the box and presented a copy of today's newspaper, flipped to the want ads. 'It says here you're looking for an office manager. Is that still the case?'

Dana blinked. 'Yes.'

Floretta smiled broadly and snapped up her box. 'Then I accept. Now, if you don't mind, I need you people to get the hell out of my space so I can get to work.'

www.ingramcontent.com/pod-product-compliance
Lightning Source LLC
Chambersburg PA
CBHW021227130626
46554CB00004B/1398